Murder by *Accident*

Bob & Claire
Enjoy!
Ken

MURDER BY *Accident*

Ken Austin

Library of Congress Control Number:		2011902038
ISBN:	Hardcover	978-1-4568-6605-1
	Softcover	978-1-4568-6604-4
	Ebook	978-1-4568-6606-8

This book was printed in the United States of America.

To order additional copies of this book, contact:

Xlibris Corporation

1-888-795-4274

www.Xlibris.com

Orders@Xlibris.com

92331

To the loving memory of my parents,
Thomas and Sarah Austin

An *accident* is a specific, identifiable, unexpected, unusual and unintended external action which occurs in a particular time and place, without apparent or deliberate cause but with marked effects. It implies a generally negative probabilistic outcome which may have been avoided or prevented had circumstances leading up to the accident been recognized, and acted upon, prior to its occurrence.

—Wikipedia, the free encyclopedia

Beloved, never avenge yourselves, but leave it to the wrath of God, for it is written, "Vengeance is mine, I will repay, says the Lord."

—Romans 12:19–21

ACKNOWLEDGMENT

While this novel and its characters are fictional, I did rely on input from numerous professionals and interested parties. I particularly want to thank the following for their contributions and counsel: Attorney Shahla M. Simpler, Dr. Constance B. Purser, Helen M. Farnan, RN, and Tara A. Penza.

And a special thank-you to my sister, Catherine Lavin, who gave hours of her time providing invaluable editing, proofing, and literary guidance.

CHAPTER ONE

It is early evening in mid-May on the verdant, becalming campus of Strafford College at North Woodlane on Long Island, New York. The sun is slowly descending, and the evening shadows are just taking shape. The campus is a beautiful sight with its ivy–speckled brick buildings, all of like architectural design. The campus is almost deserted except for the occasional faculty member and a handful of laggardly students who are racing the clock and the setting sun in getting their worldly possessions assembled and packed into their vehicles for transport home and summer storage.

Professor Randolph Anderson, at forty-three, fits the expected image and profile of a typical college professor. His tall erect stature, along with his chiseled facial features and well-styled, longish blond hair, exude a sense of bearing and wisdom. For the past five years, he has been the director of Chemical Engineering at Strafford. His only significant personality flaw is an underlying, deep-rooted sense of anger long brewing as a result of an accident that occurred when he and his twin brother, Jonathan, were eight-year-olds.

~

The twins had been swinging, side by side, on a backyard swing set at their parents' summerhouse in the Catskill Mountains in upstate New York. As the boys pumped with their legs, they rose higher and higher. Jonathan became frightened and begged Randy to slow down; instead, he kept taunting him to keep up and see how high they could go. As the swings arced upward almost to the top of the overhead horizontal support, the rear legs of the swing set pulled out of their concrete footings, casting both boys forward and off their seats. Randy fell on the side lawn and, while dazed, was unhurt. Jonathan didn't fair nearly as well. He was catapulted onto the side cement steps and was rendered unconscious. He was rushed to the town hospital by ambulance. His prognosis wasn't positive. He had sustained a severe head injury.

His first ten years after the accident were spent confined to a mental health facility in Poughkeepsie, New York. Due to his steady progress in responding to physical and pharmaceutical treatments over a ten-year period, Jonathan was transferred to Sunnyvale Meadows, a rest and rehab center near Milton, New York. His treatments were continued there through the services of his visiting medical team.

The boys' parents were horrified and raged at Randy for causing the accident, if you could really term it an accident. They felt strongly that it could have been prevented if he had acted responsibly and swung in a safe height range. Randy couldn't understand or believe their anger, and he resented their placing all the blame on him. After all, if the swing set had been properly secured in its concrete footings, the accident wouldn't have happened either. Randy would harbor that anger at his parents from then on. Anger became the ever-present cornerstone of his personality.

~

Even in his academic endeavors, Professor Anderson has to work hard at controlling his anger and temper especially when dealing with the lamer of students. He has little tolerance for irresponsibility and stupidity. Fairly regular visits to an understanding psychologist have helped tame the nasty beast, so far.

But tonight, Randolph has his mind set on other than scholastic matters. He is eagerly looking forward to tonight's recreation. It will be the last of their monthly faculty poker games of the semester. After months of losing hands and missed pots, he just knows that this will be his lucky night. He'll keep his cool and play less aggressively. And he'll have an inflated wallet to show for it at the end of the evening.

At six thirty, Randolph enters the faculty lounge in stately Harrow Hall. He and Jim Paddington, dean of the faculty, are responsible for the refreshments for tonight's card game. Quickly, they stock the lounge's refrigerator with assorted domestic and imported beer brands as well as both diet and regular canned sodas. They arrange trays of minisandwiches, pretzels, and potato chips around the large circular game table.

Charles Jensen, professor of computer science, is the senior member of the group. He has served as the official game treasurer from day one. Charles arrives and sets up the bank, exchanging dollars for chips. Peter Ryan, associate professor of mathematics, and Mike LaRusso, associate professor of chemistry, arrive, ready for action. As agreed by all at the beginning of the semester, each player selects a card from the deck and high card deals the first hand. Mike wins the honors and selects the game to be played as seven-card stud poker. He deals out the first two cards facedown to each player, and they're off.

Randolph draws pocket aces and senses a rush of good luck. He easily wins the hand and the first pot of the night. His luck holds up, and by nine o'clock, he has already won his fair share of pots; his chip stacks bear testament to his success. He is elated.

~

The chirp of his cell phone interrupts his euphoria at about nine fifteen. He sees that the call, which annoys him, is from his wife, Irene. What could she possibly want at this hour, he wonders. "Deal me out of the next few hands. I have to take this call. I'll be right back," he remarks as he rises to take the call in the hallway.

Irene, a trim comely woman of thirty-five, has been married to Randolph for ten years; they have a single child, Erin, who just turned eight. Irene has long suffered from bipolar disorder, a condition that causes her occasional mood swings, particularly if agitated.

"Are you on your way to pick up Erin from her dance lesson?" Irene asks briskly.

Realizing that he has forgotten about his agreeing to pick up Erin on his way home from the college at nine o'clock that evening, he sheepishly responds, "I'm sorry. Our faculty meeting is running a lot longer than I had expected. I totally forgot about the dance lesson. I can't possibly leave now. Rather than keeping Erin waiting for me at the dance academy, would you mind covering for me and picking her up? I'll owe you one."

Irene fumes internally but reluctantly agrees. She concludes their conversation with "Sometimes I wonder which ranks higher in your universe, your family or that damn school of yours." Randolph feels his blood pressure escalate but bites his tongue and concludes the call. He heads back to the game.

~

Irene angrily heads out to the garage, electronically opens her garage door, and gets into her late model Toyota RAV. She backs down the driveway and heads for Erin's dance academy in Garden City. It's nine twenty-five; nightfall is on its way. She should arrive at the Green Door Academy in about thirty minutes, traffic and police patrols permitting. She enters the Long Island Expressway, the main east-west corridor on Long Island. The LIE traffic is surprisingly heavy for this time of evening. Irene eases her car into the slower right-hand lane and, as soon as traffic permits, maneuvers into the fast lane. Garden City is about six exits ahead. From there, she follows North Avenue to Centre Street where she makes a right-hand turn. The academy is a few blocks ahead on the right at 648 Centre Street.

At nine fifty, Irene pulls into the academy's parking lot and eases into a convenient spot. She enters the side entrance of the academy and heads down the hall of honors—featuring a series of wall-mounted display cases hosting trophies and award cups for past academy successes. At the end of the hall, she knocks on the director's office door and enters. Mrs. Duffy, a trim, energetic forty-year-old businesswoman and the academy's lead instructor, rises to welcome her. Irene shakes her extended hand while apologizing for her tardiness, explaining the mix-up between her and her husband. Mrs. Duffy graciously accepts her explanation and proceeds to give her an assessment of Erin's progress. "Erin is one of our best students and is rapidly becoming very comfortable with the art of Irish step dancing and its rigid performance standards. Her class is rehearsing for a special exhibition of Irish dancing at the Feis, a Gaelic arts and cultural festival at Nassau Coliseum in July. They will be performing twice before hundreds of fairgoers at each show. The girls are all very excited about their first public appearance."

Irene is so proud of her daughter—a straight-A student, a well-rounded child, and a wonderful, caring daughter. She is, indeed, the very joy of Irene's life; she wishes her husband could embrace and appreciate Erin as much.

Erin comes skipping out of the studio area and greets her mother with a warm embrace and a big kiss. Bidding a good night to Mrs. Duffy, they head back down the hall of honors to the side exit. They hop into their car for the trip home. It is getting late, and Irene can't wait to get home and make some hot chocolate for Erin and herself.

~

The earlier shadows have now settled into a darkening landscape. Street lights cast eerie circular images along Centre Street. Irene reminds Erin to click on her seat belt. Conversation between mother and daughter comes easily. Hardly surprising, tonight's topic of conversation is Irish dancing and how much fun it is. Erin thanks her mother for enrolling her in the class.

As Irene turns into North Avenue, her cell phone rings. After fumbling through her large knockoff handbag, she locates the phone and speaks, "Hello, Irene here."

The caller responds, "Hi, Irene, it's Sue Greene." She was a classmate and sorority sister of Irene's at Wellesley and has remained a trusted friend and confidant over the past fifteen or so years. Sue and her husband, Dan, are Erin's godparents. "I'm afraid I have some very disturbing news to share with you. We just learned that Dan has been stricken with MS."

Irene can't believe what she just heard. She is shocked and dismayed by the terrible news. Her mind momentarily wanders off in several tangents. *Why Dan? He was always in great physical condition and exercised religiously. What would I do if Randolph were suddenly hit with something like this?*

"Oh my God, Sue, when did you find out?"

"Just this morning," replied Sue. "He had been experiencing dizziness, nausea, and muscle spasms for the last week, so we went to our internist for some answers. After reviewing Dan's symptoms and checking his vital signs, he recommended an MRI scan. We received the scan results this morning confirming advanced multiple sclerosis. Dan was admitted to Columbia Presbyterian Hospital this morning. I'm still at the hospital with Dan."

Irene's mind and emotions are racing wildly. What should she say or do? This is her best friend's husband. She again expresses her shock and sorrow. She is so caught up in the moment that her focus wavers. She doesn't assimilate the red traffic lights ahead of her—or the rapidly approaching silver sports car in the cross street to her right.

~

Chip Caruso, a recent college graduate, has spent the afternoon and early evening at the Last Call, a popular sports bar hangout for the younger set. He and his buddies are catching up on news of the local scene while hoisting a few. However, he has promised his mother he would be home early. As Chip rises to leave, he staggers a bit. His friends suggest he call a cab rather than driving himself. He won't hear of it. No way will he leave his father's Lexus RX350 silver bullet out overnight. He steadies himself and manages to get to the Lexus and drive off.

Some twenty minutes later, he is cruising along Oak Street, rapidly closing in on the North Avenue intersection. As he nears the junction, he catches a glimpse of a green car approaching from his left side. "Oh damn," he mutters as he tries to swerve his car. But it is too late to avoid the inevitable.

Erin is the first to catch sight of the speeding sports car and yells, "Mom, look out!" Shocked, Irene drops her cell phone and slams on her brakes. Both mother and daughter shriek.

The Lexus plows into the passenger side of the Toyota. The impact is horrific; the sound even worse. Both cars instantly interlock and skid across the intersection into the traffic semaphore at the northwest corner.

Both Irene and Erin are rendered unconscious by the collision; Chip is conscious but dazed. He manages to force open the passenger side door and crawl out. He can't believe his eyes. What should he do? Almost by sheer instinct, he pulls out his cell phone and calls 911. They really need help and fast.

CHAPTER TWO

Sue Greene is stunned by the ear-piercing sounds of metal crunching and human pain coming over her phone. She loses contact with Irene at the moment of impact when Irene's cell phone drops to the floor of the car.

"Hello, Irene, can you hear me?" Sue repeats over and over until she realizes it is futile. "What can I do?" she asks herself. She doesn't even know where Irene is or if anyone else is with her.

In desperation, Sue dials 911. Within seconds, her emergency call is answered. "911, how can I help you?" the dispatcher asks.

In a trembling voice, Sue explains, "My friend was just in an automobile accident. I know because I was talking with her as the accident happened. But I don't know where it happened or if anyone was injured. Can you please help me?"

"What's your name and phone number?" the dispatcher asks. "Sue Greene's my name and my cell number is 555-469-8182," replies Sue.

The dispatcher asks her to hold on while she checks their recent calls. It felt like an eternity to Sue until the dispatcher comes back on the line again.

"Hello, Mrs. Greene," the dispatcher speaks, "a call reporting an auto accident came in a few minutes ago. I don't have all of the details as yet, but I do know that an EMS team from Easton General Hospital was dispatched to the scene."

"Thank you, thank you," gushes Sue, "you're a savior." She quickly dials up Information and gets the number of Easton General. She calls and obtains the hospital's address and some general directions to get to it.

~

Sue buzzes for Dan's nurse and explains her dilemma. She has to leave Dan's side for a few hours to attend to a dear friend who was just in a serious auto accident. The nurse assures Sue that Dan is in good hands and that they are monitoring his every breath. Reassured, Sue kisses Dan on his cheek and heads out to her car. She follows her directions to Easton General Hospital.

~

On the other side of town, two police cars arrive at the crash scene. One patrol car crew proceeds to cordon off the entire intersection using traffic stanchions and sparking red flares. The other team addresses the victims of the accident. Working around the deflated and powder-covered front air bags, Officer Ralph Adams checks both Irene and Erin for their visible condition and vital life signs. He immediately calls for backup and an ambulance. He remains with Irene and Erin until the ambulance arrives.

Officer Frank Magill begins his accident report with a sketch of the accident scene including the apparent driving direction of both vehicles, before and after impact. He also walks off each car's skid marks and braking distances.

Officer Matt Baggins interrogates the other involved driver, Charles Caruso Jr. and checks his credentials. Suspecting that he has been drinking, Officer Baggins reads him his rights and offers to administer a Breath Analysis Test (BAT) to determine his blood-alcohol concentration (BAC). Caruso agrees to the test. His BAC measures .016, twice the threshold level indicating intoxication. Baggins cites Caruso for driving under the influence (DUI) and reckless driving. He cuffs Chip and settles him in the rear of his patrol car for the eventual trip to the police station.

Officer Magill catalogues the contents of both cars and places them in separate sealed evidence bags. They will be taken to the police station and secured in the evidence room. He then issues Irene a citation for reckless driving.

The EMS ambulance arrives, and the technicians spring into action. The women are carefully extradited from their vehicle and secured on mobile ambulance cots for transportation to Easton General Hospital. Their vital signs are rechecked; Irene has regained consciousness but is still a bit delirious. She has a severe contusion on her right thigh.

Erin is unconscious and judged to be in very serious condition with head contusions, bleeding, and multiple bone fractures. Erin and her mother are carefully fitted with temporary cervical collars to stabilize their necks and heads for their trip to the hospital. The EMS ambulance speeds off to nearby Easton General with sirens whining.

Chip is taken to the Easton police station where he is officially booked and arraigned for DUI and reckless driving causing serious injury. The initial charge of reckless driving was amended when the extent of Erin's injuries became known. Irene's citation was also amended.

The duty officer that evening is Lt. James Neef. Reviewing the booking documents, he recognizes a familiar name and asks the young man if he is related to Charles Caruso, the head of Caruso Construction. "Yes, sir, that's my father," the young man replies. He provides Lt. Neef with his family's home phone number.

As a professional courtesy to Mr. Caruso, a well-known and respected figure of the Long Island community, Lt. Neef places a call to the Caruso residence. He introduces himself and informs Mr. Caruso that his son has been involved in an auto collision that sent two women to Easton General Hospital in serious condition. While his son is in good physical shape, he is being charged with a DUI and reckless driving. Apparently, he had been drinking with some of his schoolmates during the afternoon.

Mr. Caruso is the sole owner and president of Caruso Construction Company, one of Long Island's most successful and prominent commercial construction companies. They're involved in many municipal, state, and federal construction projects and are well recognized. Mr. Caruso is quite involved in the political and social scene on Long Island, being a generous contributor of time and funds to charitable causes as well as to political campaigns.

Upon hearing the disturbing news, Charles Caruso immediately calls his company counsel, Donald Langsford, at his home even though it was almost eleven o'clock. After passing on what little information he knows, he asks Langsford to visit his son in jail that evening and advise him how to handle matters. He particularly wants Landsford to caution Chip about talking with anyone without counsel present and to refuse to submit to any blood or urine testing. Caruso then asks Langsford to call him at his office on his way home to fill him in on the situation.

Caruso then wakens his wife, Carmella, and tells her the upsetting news. He consoles her and asks her not to talk to anyone about the accident, particularly anyone from the media. He tells Carmella that he is now heading off to his office to work on the situation from there. He assures his wife he will take good care of their only son. He gives her a reassuring kiss on the cheek and heads off to his office.

~

Within thirty minutes, Caruso is perched in his favorite padded chair behind a weathered oak desk. For the past twenty-five years, it has been the control center of his universe. This is where he will orchestrate this latest challenge.

His first call is to their auto insurance agent to report the accident. The second call is to Charlie "Coco" Crandel, a retired NYC policeman turned private investigator. He was retired ten years ago due to a service disability. While on the force, Coco earned his nickname for his penchant for crisp, stylish attire.

Caruso Construction has employed his services often over the years on varied assignments from personnel theft cases to construction related disputes. Coco also served as an expert witness in company litigation. Caruso was always most pleased with his work. Coco was discreet but effective. And he was always available 24/7 via a special cell phone number. Caruso places the call.

Sure enough, Coco answers the call on the third buzz. Caruso explains his son's predicament to Coco. Obviously, prompt action is required. Caruso needs him to immediately contact the best available accident reconstruction and investigation firm. They must get started soon before the accident scene becomes contaminated. They will investigate and analyze the circumstances and particulars of the accident to determine a probable cause of the accident as well as all other contributing factors. Their report and possible testimony will serve as the linchpin of his son's defense.

"Also, Coco, I also need the latest health report on the two females in the other car involved in the accident," continued Caruso. "They're at Easton General Hospital and their last name is Anderson. Put a rush on this, Coco. Their physical condition could play a critical role in how our case is handled."

~

The EMS ambulance comes screeching to a halt at the ER entrance to Easton General. The ER personnel are prepared for their arrival and rush out to expedite the patients' transfer to their trauma center. The EMS had alerted them to their condition and estimated arrival time. Several triage nurses examine both patients and confirm the EMS team's preliminary diagnoses. Irene is the least urgent and is assigned to an adjacent examination room; Erin's serious condition necessitates an urgent call to the staff surgeon on duty.

After the surgeon's evaluation, Erin is rushed to the OR for immediate life-saving surgery to stem several oozing hematomas in her head.

Irene, while still woozy, is treated for the major laceration on her right thigh. Multiply stitches are required. The area is swabbed with a sterile solution and well bandaged.

Once the wound treatment is completed, Irene requests a telephone to inform her husband of the accident and its aftermath.

"Oh my God," mutters Randolph as he hears the news. "How did it happen?"

A shaken Irene snaps back, "You didn't pick Erin up after her dance lesson."

Randolph holds his temper and his tongue and asks where she and Erin are. He then asks to speak to a nurse so he can get the latest condition report for both Irene and Erin. The head nurse advises Randolph that Irene appears to be unnerved by the accident but is okay, excepting her leg wound. They will, however, keep her overnight as a precaution.

His daughter, Erin, is in very serious condition with broken bones and severe damage to her head and brain. She is presently in surgery.

After completing the phone call, Randolph hurriedly packs an overnight case for Irene and speeds off to the hospital.

~

Charles Caruso answers the private phone line in his office. "Hi, it's me, Donald. I just left Chip, and he's in good condition, both physically and emotionally. I was able to arrange for his bail. He'll be released later this morning. I'll follow up on that to make sure it happens. By the way, have you thought about getting an accident reconstruction analysis and report? It might prove to be our strongest defense weapon as we move forward."

Charles responds, "Yes, that's already in the works. Get some sleep. I'll talk with you later today. And, Donald, thanks."

~

Randolph Anderson and Sue Greene arrive at the hospital within minutes of each other. She sees him in the ER emergency reception area and goes over and gives him a hug and a greeting. They ask to visit with Irene and are directed to room 6C in the ER overnight wing. Randolph also requests that the head nurse meet them in room 6C to advise them on Erin's condition and prognosis.

In her hospital room, Irene greets Sue warmly with an enthusiastic embrace and her husband with a tepid hello.

The head ER nurse, Janet Johnson, arrives and begins, "We're moderately optimistic about Erin's long-term prognosis. Our surgical team is still conducting tests to pinpoint specific failings. She suffered severe trauma to her head and brain. Until they complete their tests and preliminary surgery, we can't be more specific." She continues, "We will keep you informed on her progress on a regular basis."

"One last question," asks Randolph. "Can I stay someplace close to Erin overnight?" Nurse Johnson replies, "Actually it would be better for all concerned if you went home and got a good night's sleep. Everything here is under control for tonight."

They thank Nurse Johnson for her concern and help.

With Irene slowly fading into a state of total sleep, Sue leaves and heads back to check on Dan. Randolph decides to stay for a few more hours.

CHAPTER THREE

Page three of the *N.Y. Daily Journal* features an eye-catching headline and follow-up article:

DRUNKEN YOUTH CAUSES NEAR FATAL ACCIDENT
Girl in Serious Condition in Hospital

> The article identifies the male DUI as 22 year old Charles Caruso Jr., son of business magnate Charles Caruso of Harborport, L.I. Mr. Caruso is President of Caruso Construction Company. The article also identifies the female victim as eight year old Erin Anderson, daughter of Professor and Mrs. Randolph Anderson. Professor Anderson is Director of Chemical Engineering at Strafford College.

~

Jonathan Anderson, in his enlightened state of mind, has acquired an interest in the local news and the world beyond the walls of Sunnyvale Meadows. Whenever possible, he ambles over to the recreation center and scans the headlines of the *Daily Journal* and the *New York Times* for items of interest to him. This morning, the DUI headline and article piques his interest. He wonders if the mentioned Randolph Anderson could be

Randy, his despised twin brother. It would be just like him to be involved in perpetrating misery on yet another eight-year-old. He has to find out for sure.

~

Sue Greene calls Irene's hospital room the next morning. Irene, still in a semihaze, answers the call with a cautious hello. Sue responds, "Irene, it's me. How are you this morning? I am just leaving Dan's hospital and heading over to see you and Erin. Dan will be undergoing diagnostic evaluations all morning, so I have the time. I thought we could also check you out of the hospital this morning. Then I'll drive you home and get you settled, if you like."

"Sounds good, Sue," answers Irene. "Thanks for being such a great friend, especially with all that's going on in your life."

"Fine, I'll see you in about an hour." When Irene hangs up, she rings the nurses' station and requests a wheelchair so she will be ready for a visit with Sue to Erin in the ICU.

Sue arrives at the hospital and rushes up to Irene's room. They hug and kiss. Then they head up to the ICU to visit with Erin.

Erin's condition hasn't changed noticeably since yesterday. She is still comatose, and her breathing is labored, even with a ventilator assist. Irene and Sue can only see Erin's closed eyes through her head cast and bandages. Irene mutters a fervent prayer and wishes that she could change places with her precious little lamb. She starts sobbing.

The attending nurse attempts to console Irene by mentioning that Erin came through the previous night's surgery and procedures in good order. She concludes with "Her vital signs remain steady. The next thirty-six hours will be crucial."

Irene continues to sob. The nurse draws her close and embraces her. The nurse eases her away from Erin's bed and assures Irene that Erin is being carefully monitored.

Irene thanks the nurse and asks Sue to wheel her back to her room. The thought that Randolph might very well have prevented this catastrophe again flashes through her consciousness.

Once back in Irene's room, Sue helps her get dressed and packed. They check out of the hospital. Irene is wheeled out to Sue's car and off they go. They agree to pick up some light fare on the way to Irene's house and have lunch. During lunch, Irene opens up to Sue regarding her feelings of betrayal by Randolph and his complicity in this terrible tragedy. She says, "I don't know if I will ever get over it." Sue is very simpatico with Irene's feelings. She too came to the same conclusion and also laid much of the blame on Randolph's shoulders. Maybe this staunch attitude is a subconscious attempt to mitigate her own deep frustration with her husband's terminal prognosis.

Irene tells Sue that she is going to make an appointment with her long-term family doctor to discuss her twisted thoughts and desire for vengeance. Perhaps Dr. Jensen will be able to advise her as to what she should or could do to navigate these troubled waters. Sue agrees that it's a good first step.

~

Charles Caruso arranges for a meeting at his office with Coco Crandel, his PI, and Donald Langsford, his attorney, to review the accident reconstruction investigation report that Coco just received. It will help Charles decide on a course of action for the looming legal struggle.

The comprehensive investigation report is accompanied by numerous graphs, maps, and photographs. After leading Charles and Donald through the report, Coco concludes that:

- The driver of car no. 1 (Mrs. Anderson) was on her cell phone to a Susan Greene for approximately five minutes before the moment of impact.
- Car no. 1's skid pattern was sixty-four feet from initial braking to the point of impact, indicating a top speed of sixty-eight miles per hour. The posted speed limit along North Avenue is thirty-five miles per hour.
- Car no.1 ran a red light at the point-of-impact intersection. The violation occurred at 9:13 PM and is documented by official overhead red light cameras.
- Car no. 1's skid pattern varied little from start to finish, indicating almost no effort to avoid a collision by veering away from car no. 2 (Chip Caruso).
- Car no. 2's skid-pattern-measured length was ninety-eight feet, indicating a top speed of fifty-nine miles per hour. The posted speed limit on Oak Street is forty-five miles per hour.
- Car no. 2's skid pattern at mile marker sixty-three feet began a progressive directional adjustment to the right to avoid car no. 1.

The report concluded with an estimation of comparative and contributing negligence for each party/car of 68 percent for car no. 1 and 32 percent for car no. 2.

This negligence assessment was based on the studied conclusion that the driver of car no. 1 was appreciably distracted by the cell phone call she received just prior to the crash. Car no.1 was exceeding the posted speed limit by thirty-three miles per hour or 94.3 percent while car no. 2 was exceeding the speed limit by fourteen miles per hour or 31.1 percent. And importantly, car no.1 ignored the red light signal at the impact intersection.

A normal reaction in this circumstance on the part of car no.1's driver might have prevented this collision.

Being that New York State is a pure-comparative-fault state, this negligence assessment would result in a finding that car no. 2 would only be responsible for 32 percent of any possible monetary judgment.

The report also presented findings as to the accuracy of the particular Breath Analysis Test unit (EDP # 671-384D) employed by the police in this case. This unit was last calibrated for accuracy on November 4 of last year. The BAT manufacturer requires the return of each field machine every six months for factory calibration.

The BAT readings in this case are unreliable since the unit wasn't calibrated on schedule as required.

All parties are pleased and impressed with the comprehensiveness of the investigative report. Charles speaks first, "Good job, Coco. Now we have something substantive to build our case around. And we also have Chip's driving record to extol. He has been driving for almost five years now and has never been ticketed for any driving offense, including parking. Chip is a good, conscientious driver."

Donald adds, "This comprehensive report and Chip's stellar driving record will serve us well in drafting our response to the court. Our plan is to file a motion with the court to suppress the Breath Analysis Test results due to the failure of the police department to properly service the test equipment as required by the manufacturer.

"Once we have successfully had those test results invalidated, we will file a motion to dismiss the DUI charge and amend the felony reckless driving causing serious injury charge to a misdemeanor charge of reckless driving."

Charles is visibly pleased with the efforts of his investigative and legal teams. He thanks them, and they depart.

~

"How horrible that headline 'Drunken Youth Causes Near Fatal Accident.' It's even worse when you consider that none of this had to happen. Why can't youngsters understand the wicked power of alcohol? They're only interested in guzzling hard liquor with their cronies with little regard for the possible effects of their thoughtlessness. In this case, a beautiful young girl is their victim. I hope that the authorities make this selfish young man pay a substantial price for his recklessness."

~

Chip's DUI case is the first time the Caruso family has had an encounter with the criminal court system in their family's long history in the United States.

Charles's wife, Carmella, is a first-generation American. Her father, Joseph Roselli, and her mother, Marie D'Amici, were childhood friends in the rural little Italian town of Tremizzo along the shore of beautiful Lake Como in the Lombardy region of northern Italy. The area is noted for its flower growing and harvesting, particularly azaleas and rhododendrons. Perhaps that accounts for Carmella's green thumb and love of flowers.

Separately, Joseph Roselli and Marie D'Amici immigrated to the United States in the late '30s to avoid the inevitable curse of Mussolini's fascism. The couple met again in the little Italy section of lower Manhattan in New York, and they married in 1946, right after Joseph returned home from serving in the US Army in World War II. The Rosellis had five children; Carmella was the middle child being born in 1957. The family settled in the northern New Jersey town of Bergenfield.

Carmella met Charles through mutual friends, and after dating for almost five years, they were married in 1982. Chip was born in 1988, and his sister, Cara, joined the family in 2002.

Charles's parents, Anthony and Roberta, were native-born Americans. Charles was the oldest of three children. His father developed a successful residential plumbing business in the Bedford section of Brooklyn, New York. Anthony and Roberta were very proud of Charles; he was the first member of the family to graduate from college. He received a BS in civil engineering from New York University.

Charles's grandparents, Pasquale and Rose, came to the United States in the late 1890s and settled in the Lower East Side of Manhattan. He worked as a handyman/laborer, and Rose took in laundry to make ends meet. They had two children, Anthony and Teresa.

Charles apparently inherited his father's business drive and determination. Applying these talents, he steadily developed his commercial contracting business. The result was a profitable enterprise that provided the Caruso family a comfortable upper class lifestyle with all its amenities.

~

PI Coco Crandel pays a visit to Charlie Hagerty, a longtime friend and associate. They served together on the NYPD at the ninth precinct in lower Manhattan. Since retirement three years ago, Charlie has worked part-time as a security guard at Easton General Hospital.

They meet and exchange manly hugs. Coco explains about the accident and the importance of his client knowing the day-to-day condition and prognosis of one of the hospital's ICU patients by the name of Erin Anderson.

Charlie agrees to contact a key nurse in the ICU ward that he knows well and obtain a daily report on Erin. Coco will call him every afternoon an hour after Charlie reports for work. Coco assures Charlie that he will take care of him and his nurse contact as the case progresses.

Coco thanks Charlie for his big assist and shakes his hand. They smile and Coco leaves. Coco will pass this medical update to Donald Langsford's office each day.

~

Donald Langsford reviews the two motions and the plea bargain that his firm developed for submission to the court on behalf of Chip Caruso. The first motion is requesting dismissal of the DUI charge due to the police department's failure to have the BAT test equipment calibrated on schedule, as required.

The second motion requests that the reckless-driving-causing-serious-injury felony charge be amended to a misdemeanor charge of reckless driving due to the dismissal of the DUI charge.

The third brief is a proposal prepared for Charles Caruso Jr.'s signature to plead guilty to this amended misdemeanor charge of reckless driving with a $2,000 fine, a ninety-day restriction on his driver's license to daytime hours, his enrollment in the DMV's alcohol education and prevention program, and one year's probation.

Armed with these documents, Langsford contacts Charles Caruso to arrange for a meeting with him and his son to review all the elements of the case as well as the latest motions and a plea-bargain option. They agree to meet at Charles's office on Thursday of this week at two o'clock. When Charles calls Chip to tell him of the meeting, Chip responds with "How long will it take?" Furious at such a response, he replies, "We could just forget the whole matter and let you deal with it on your own."

CHAPTER FOUR

Randolph Anderson visits the hospital every day and spends several hours at Erin's bedside. As he reflects about the past few days, he keeps trying to convince himself that he was not complicit in causing this horrible accident. His only relief comes when he can place the entire guilty yoke on the shoulders of that young drunken driver, Chip Caruso. *He's probably another one of those pampered, rich brats like so many of his students. They're all about me, me, me. If that bum hadn't been drinking that day, my little girl would be home with us today and not in this hospital. I hate that kid. I wish he was lying here instead of my sweet Erin*. He sighs.

Try as he may to dispel them, Randolph still has serious recriminations about many aspects of this catastrophe. It really wasn't a true accident, was it? That Caruso boy was the perpetrator. He is responsible. He will carry the heavy yoke of guilt forever.

But wait, didn't he, himself, contribute to this tragedy by not fulfilling his promise to pick up his daughter that night? He's a better driver than his wife, particularly at night. And his Cadillac Escalade is built stronger than her RAV4. Plus it has reinforced side panels and side air bags. It probably could have withstood the side impact of that collision.

On his way home from the hospital, Randolph stops by a car rental agency and arranges for a rental car for Irene until their automobile insurance company settles their accident claim. He selects a midnight blue Chevrolet sedan.

~

Sue Greene visits her husband, Dan, at Columbia Presbyterian Hospital the next morning. She is shocked at the level of his overnight deterioration. He is in severe pain and can hardly move about in his bed. Even his speech is garbled and hard to understand. It's unbelievable. She rushes out to the nurses' station and asks for his nurse, Martha Henry. When she appears, she sheepishly says, "Hello, Mrs. Greene. I'm glad you came in this morning. We have to talk. Let's go over to the patients' lounge, and I'll fill you in on your husband's condition."

In the lounge, she begins, "I'm sorry to have to inform you that your husband's MS is a very progressive substrain. He is in a subgroup of about 10 to 15 percent of MS victims that don't experience any substantive periods of remission. This strain causes victims to experience steady neurologic declines and suffer constant attacks. I know it's terrible news to hear. But we have to be realistic in cases like this."

Sue tries gallantly to absorb this incredulous news, but she finally does succumb and cries. Nurse Martha attempts to console her by holding her close and rubbing her back while uttering comforting words, "There, there, it's good for you to let it out. Take your time, Mrs. Greene."

In time, Sue recovers her bearings and thanks Martha for being so supportive. It's never easy to have to pass on bad news. But she wonders why this had to happen to Dan. And selfishly, why did it have to happen to her?

~

It's Thursday afternoon, and Donald Langsford arrives at Charles's office for their consult on Chip's DUI case. Chip arrives ten minutes after two. To keep the atmosphere businesslike, Charles ushers them into his executive conference room. Charles sits at the head of the conference table with Donald and Chip at opposite sides.

Donald begins, "I'm here today to bring everyone up to speed on the case and its developments. I will lay out our progress to date and hopefully set our game plan as we move forward. I just received the latest medical update on Erin Anderson's condition in the ICU ward at Easton General. She is still comatose with no other changes in her vegetative state. Her prognosis remains grim. There's no telling how long she will survive. God bless her."

"We must have our case adjudicated before she passes on. Obviously, the stakes elevate in a case like this if a fatality, especially of a young girl, is involved."

Charles and Chip nod their understanding of the case and its ramifications. Langsford continues, "Chip, as you probably know, your father commissioned a well-respected automobile accident investigatory firm to evaluate all the factors involved in this accident to help assign blame or culpability on all parties to the accident on a proportional basis."

He adds, "We also have the benefit of the professional services of Caruso Construction's valued private investigator, Coco Crandel, to nose around to see what he might be able to uncover to foster our case. He's already paid dividends by making contact with an inside party at Erin's hospital to keep us abreast of her condition and prognosis on a daily basis."

Langsford then reviews the accident investigatory company's report with Charles and Chip. He concludes the recap with "As you can see there are numerous mitigating factors which favor our position."

He continues, "Coco was also able to secure a printout of Erin's mother's cell phone log for the day of the accident. It proves that Irene Anderson was on her cell phone minutes before the collision with a Susan Greene. We know she had to have been distracted by that call. We've amassed and attached significant authoritative research studies that convincingly prove that cell phone use while driving does cause driver distraction."

Langsford reviews the two motions his firm has prepared for submission to the court. One is for the DUI charge dismissal based on the faulty BAT test equipment. The other addresses the amending of the reckless-driving felony charge to a less-serious reckless-driving misdemeanor charge.

He then details the plea bargain that his firm is suggesting be submitted for the court's consideration. Chip asks for more details on his driver's license restrictions and how it works.

Langsford explains, "The courts usually suspend one's driver's license for ninety days for first offenders, no exceptions. We're arguing that such a suspension would deny you an opportunity to earn a living. With our daylight exception, you will be able to use your car during the day. Our goal is to avoid a DUI conviction which would stigmatize you forever. And, as important, to resolve your case while the Anderson girl is still alive."

Charles interjects, "It all makes sense to me. You and your firm have done a fine job to date. We have to move along as fast as we can while time is on our side. Chip, I hope you can see the merits in all of this, especially the plea bargain."

Chip halfheartedly nods his head and utters, "Sure, yeah sure."

Charles flushes at Chip's lame acknowledgment and looks at Donald. "Thanks again for a job well done. Keep me informed."

Donald Langsford packs up, shakes everyone's hand, and leaves.

Charles looks over at Chip and sternly says, "We have to talk."

~

Separately, Irene and Randolph Anderson consult with their long-term family doctor, Dr. Jerome Jensen, about their family crisis and their feelings of recrimination, vengeance, and sorrow. After a lengthy discussion with each of them, he suggests professional counseling or the joining of a grief bereavement group to help resolve their myriad and entangled issues. Irene silently dismisses the suggestion of counseling but decides to look into joining a local bereavement group or MADD, the advocacy organization of mothers against drunk driving.

In his session with Irene, Dr. Jensen asks her about her mood swings, "Have you noticed any dramatic increase in the number and intensity of these mood swings since the accident?" Irene admits that they have intensified but seem to be manageable. Dr. Jensen advises Irene to come back in if she feels that things are getting out of control. Irene agrees and leaves his office.

Randolph will follow up with Dr. Ramon Stevenson, a clinical psychologist whom he has been seeing for the past ten years or so in dealing with his birth family issues and his resident anger.

~

Irene meets with a nearby bereavement group; she finds that their focus is mostly directed at overcoming the loss of a loved one. Her issues go deeper than that; she is also dealing with hatred, blame, suspicion, and vengeance. MADD seems to more closely deal with the accident, its causes, and aftermath.

Irene selects MADD and decides to join and start attending sessions. Her goal is to learn to reconcile her feelings of self-blame in not avoiding the accident and her despise of her husband for placing his interests before those of his family. She still is having difficulty dealing with all the "what-ifs" of the situation.

~

The law firm of Langsford and Reynolds submits their two motion briefs, via special messenger, to the prosecutor's office, attention Assistant District Attorney Joseph Tangradi who has been assigned the prosecution of the Caruso DUI case.

Once they receive hopefully favorable responses to their two motions, Donald Langsford will contact ADA Tangradi to arrange for a pretrial conference to discuss his firm's proposals for a possible plea bargain on the amended charges. This process could take anywhere from a few weeks to a month or more. ADA Tangradi will have to interview all the police officers involved and get their take on the incident. He will also have to review the details of the case with the DA's own accident investigatory team and consider their recommendations.

~

After much consideration, Irene attends her first MADD session. She hopes that the women in the organization can help her dispel her constant thoughts of vengeance and retribution. Irene is enthusiastically welcomed and soon is participating in the evening's group discussions. At the end of those interchanges, everyone is given time to address the group and open a new discussion topic. Irene seizes the opportunity.

Irene tries to explain her inner feelings of sadness, guilt, and the desire for revenge. After hearing all about her daughter and her plight, her selfish husband, his despised twin brother, and the accident, the panel offers some preliminary suggestions for Irene's consideration, including the following:

- Contact her husband's twin brother to see if he can provide Irene with some insight into her husband's twisted psyche.
- Counsel with a close friend who would be more understanding of her issues and feelings.
- Seek an outlet for her intense energy, perhaps a job or a hobby.
- Report back on her progress at a future meeting.

Irene is very pleased with the MADD group. She can see how they may be able to really help her deal with her myriad unwanted feelings. But first, she has to see her baby back to health.

~

Sue calls Irene and invites her to lunch at a local luncheonette. During their meal, Irene tells Sue about her MADD experience at her first meeting.

"They listened to my story intently and then suggested some very positive steps that I could consider to get through my anger and revenge issues. Perhaps you would like to join me at their next meeting. I'm sure you would also benefit from their counsel. They get into so many other issues beyond just drinking and driving."

Sue smiles and says, "I'd love to tag along with you. You know, Irene, I never mentioned this to you before, but I feel a heavy onus is on me for distracting you right before the accident. I should have waited until you got home to pass on such a jarring message. I also despise that Caruso kid for drinking and driving that night."

The ladies continue to stroke each other's wounded psyches throughout lunch and eventually part company with a big meaningful hug and kiss.

Sue rushes back to Columbia Presbyterian Hospital to visit with her husband and check on his current condition. She is not very optimistic after hearing that dire prognosis from his nurse yesterday. But Dan has snapped back from other health issues before. She prays silently that he will pull through once again although she realizes in this case the odds are really stacked against him.

~

When Professor Anderson arrives home, there is a FedEx package from Strafford College waiting for him at his front door. It contains course materials for the two summer session courses that he is scheduled to teach plus a preliminary student roster for each course. Also included are two copies of the five required reading textbooks and their syllabi. The second set is for any associate who might assist him with the classroom work. The course and textbooks are

> #CE-13R Global Warming, a study regarding the present debate over global warming and its projected future repercussions. Required reading:
>
> > *An Inconvenient Truth: The Planetary Emergency* by Albert A. Gore Jr.
> >
> > *The Truth About the Global Warming Threat* by Ralph R. Sampson, PhD

#CE-68R Applied Toxicology 101, identification and analysis of toxic elements in the world around us. Required reading:

Toxins and the Environment by Dr. Ronald C. Dapper
Your Home and its Toxicology by John A. Hagerty, PhD
Green Toxicology by Professor Calvin B. Boehme

It doesn't take Randolph long to engulf himself in this welcomed project. It will help divert his mind from its present state of despair and anger.

He takes the package into his study and opens it. He begins the arduous but pleasing process of digesting and absorbing all five texts. While reading each of the books, he starts making incisive notes and references on lined five-by-seven-inch index cards. Each card will be edited and refined several times; eventually, they will morph into his lecture guides for each of his courses.

Randolph prefers to reference these precise but discreet lecture guides in class than rely on reading from the textbooks. He believes this approach to lecturing conveys an impression of serious personal preparation of the class work to his students, thereby hopefully motivating them.

~

Following up on one of the MADD group's suggestions, Irene applies for and accepts a position as a customer service representative for SunnySide Foods, a major consumer food products company. The territory involved in this position encompasses all Nassau and Suffolk counties, effectively including all of Long Island, New York.

Irene's job will be to follow up on all consumer concerns or complaints with any of the company's food products. Her mission is to placate upset consumers, thereby obviating the threat of any legal action or negative press against the company and to create goodwill.

Irene will work three days a week (Monday, Wednesday, and Friday), eight hours a day, portal-to-portal. She will drive her own car and be reimbursed on a per mile basis, plus expenses.

The very thought of performing a mind-challenging function already has provided a welcome buffer from her present numbing mindset. Irene is very enthused at this opportunity and can't wait for her in-office training to begin.

CHAPTER FIVE

Randolph and Jonathan Anderson's grandfather, James, was a pioneer in the nascent frozen food industry; he developed much of the early quick-freeze technology. His firm was eventually purchased by the Bird's Eye Company in the midthirties. His son, Martin, Randolph's father, joined him at that point. Together they formed a food distribution company that specialized in servicing institutional clients nationwide.

As a result of these business successes, the families enjoyed an elevated standard of living through the years.

When Jonathan experienced his unfortunate fall from the swing set and sustained serious brain damage, his father arranged for the finest of medical care and treatment.

Jonathan's father also set up a trust fund for him to cover his residential and medical expenses and to provide him a generous monthly stipend for sundry personal expenses.

In recent years, due to his steady and marked medical improvement, particularly in his cognitive skills, his medical advisors agreed to grant Jonathan the freedom to travel off-campus several days each month. The center's staff is amazed at the uptick in his mood and responsiveness with this new option. Over time, the staff does wonder where Jonathan goes during his sojourns. All they know is that he takes the Sunnyvale courtesy jitney to town in the morning and returns the same way later the same day. There were never any negative comments received from anyone in town, so the trips continue.

~

Following up on another suggestion offered at her last MADD meeting, Irene decides to visit with Jonathan, her husband's twin brother, to see if she can uncover any insights into Randolph's dark side. Although Randolph never had any relationship with his twin after the accident, the family did get updated medical reports from time to time. Irene has read some of these updates that were sent to Randolph and knows about the progress Jonathan had made. Perhaps meeting Jonathan might also help her resolve some of her own mixed feelings for her husband.

Irene calls Sunnyvale Meadows and speaks with the director. She explains her relationship to Jonathan Anderson and her hope of meeting with him. The director informs Irene that Jonathan himself must pass on all visitors; he agrees to clear her visit with Jonathan and get back to her.

Later that afternoon, Irene receives a return call from the director's assistant informing her that Jonathan would be pleased to meet with her. She sets the time and date for their face-to-face.

At the appointed time, Irene enters Sunnyvale Meadows and walks up to the reception desk and announces herself. She is directed to Jonathan's suite.

She is surprised at the ambiance and casualness of the facility; she was expecting more of an asylum arrangement with uniformed guards and restricted access. Instead, she finds Sunnyvale more like an upscale residence hotel.

Jonathan is expecting her and rises from a comfortable-looking stuffed armchair to greet her. Irene is amazed at the likeness of Jonathan to her husband. They are indeed identical twins. The only discernible difference is Jonathan's blond crew cut hairdo. Irene hands Jonathan a recent color picture of Randolph and comments, "Except for your different hairdos, you truly are identical." Jonathan is equally amazed at their likeness.

After some preliminary small talk, Irene soon realizes the depth of Jonathan's disdain for his brother. He still blames Randy, as he calls him, for the swing set accident and his subsequent medical problems. As far as Jonathan is concerned, it is really pretty simple: Randy stole his youth from him.

Although Jonathan travels off-campus several times each month, Jonathan never visits or contacts any member of his family that cast him aside years ago. Some family members have attempted telephone contact over the years, but Jonathan would have nothing to do with them.

Toward the end of their hour-long visit, Jonathan raises the issue of the car accident. Irene is surprised at this disclosure and says, "I didn't know you knew of it."

"Yes," explains Jonathan. "I read about it in some of the local papers." He tells Irene that the taking of Erin's youth reminds him of his own experience. "At least I have made some progress and have hope for the future."

Irene opens up a bit to Jonathan and admits she actually blames Randolph for the circumstances that led up to the accident. She explains about Randolph's forgetting about his pickup of Erin that night after her dance lesson. "I just know," declares Irene, "that Erin would be alive today if he had done what he had promised that night."

"I guess you and I have quite a bit in common," Jonathan remarks. He adds, "Randy is evil, he was responsible for both catastrophes. Both really were nonaccidents and should be avenged."

Irene is somewhat surprised by his response but gives no clue. This is something she will have to ponder on her own. Before leaving Jonathan, Irene asks Jonathan if he would be interested in being picked up Thursday morning at eleven o'clock for an interesting car ride out to Long Island to grab a firsthand look at the Carusos' estate house.

Jonathan's spirits are buoyed. He quickly accepts the offer. Ever since he heard of the wealthy Carusos, he's wanted to know more about them.

Awkwardly, he rises and reaches out to hug her. When she responds favorably, Jonathan thanks her profusely for her visit. Irene smiles and utters, "See you on Thursday." As Irene drives back home, she wonders if she married the wrong twin.

~

Sue decides to join Irene at her next evening MADD meeting. Sue will meet Irene at the MADD offices after spending the day with Dan. Irene introduces her friend to the group before explaining that she had followed their recommendation and made contact with her husband's twin brother, Jonathan.

"I actually visited him at the residence home where he lives," explains Irene. "He holds a deep and long-term disdain for his twin, my husband. It all goes back to that backyard swing set accident when they were eight years old. Jonathan still blames my husband both for the accident and his lost youth."

Irene continues, "Surprisingly, Jonathan had heard about the automobile accident and was curious about the circumstances. I explained about the mix-up between Randolph and me regarding picking up Erin that night after her dance lesson. I could see Jonathan's face redden and his nostrils flare as he considered his brother's role in the accident scenario."

Irene adds, "Jonathan asked me how my little girl was doing. I explained that Erin was still in a coma at the hospital." "That bastard," he blustered, "he could have prevented this whole disaster if he had acted like a man. He hasn't changed a bit over the years."

Sue was very impressed with Irene's presentation and initiative before the MADD group. After the meeting, she asks Irene, "Could I go along with you the next time you visit Jonathan? I'd really appreciate it."

"You're on, I'll let you know when" is Irene's smiling reply.

~

Charles Caruso is a classic-car buff. In the Carusos' four-car garage, there's reserved parking for Charles's '54 restored Chevy Bel Air powder blue convertible, his '49 restored Chevy fastback sedan, his new silver Lexus RX 350 crossover company car now in the body shop and Carmella's Honda Prelude. Charles loves driving the '54 Chevy on pleasant weekends in the spring and summer. For social or business occasions, he relies on the Lexus. Following the classic car market via auctions has been his hobby for many years. While he limits his collection to a few cars, he relishes the rush from bidding on a relic, the exhilaration of winning, and then the joy of restoration. He has shelved any dreams of expanding his stable until his Lexus is restored to better than new condition.

While Chip is without wheels, his mother kindly gives him the keys to her Prelude for limited use. She will drive the loaner car. With the summer weather so delightful, Charles cheerfully drives either his '49 Chevy or his '54 Bel Air convertible to and from work each day. He relishes the many ogles his cars receive each day.

Carmella couldn't care less about cars, new or old. Her passion is her garden. She finds great solace in tending to her beautiful miniature nursery on the right side of their home. This year she is cultivating peonies, irises, and rhododendrons. Each species is planted in parallel rows of twenty-five deep, each carefully staked and secured with ties. The entire nursery is encased by a classic white metal picket fence which can be electrified to deter predators of all kinds. The entire showcase is girded by a marble stone walkway for aesthetic reasons and for the benefit of curious neighbors and visitors. Carmella is so proud of her living creation. She spends hours each week weeding, cultivating, and overall, tending to her "baby."

~

As a diversion from the disturbing events of the past month, Charles suggests that the entire family get away from their present surroundings for a few days. He recommends a three-day rehab at their summer home in Stony Pines, about an hour's drive east of Harborport. It would give them all some valuable family time together and a chance to reset their priorities.

Chip begs off the excursion, citing a previous Fordham alumni activity. His mother and father are not pleased.

After dinner, the packing begins. Within a few hours, everyone is pretty well-set for the trip. They will get going early tomorrow after breakfast.

Carmella asks her good friend and neighbor, Janet Zook, to watch over her precious nursery for a few days while she is gone. All Janet has to do is walk through the nursery every day and pluck any sprouting weeds. Janet readily accepts the assignment.

Next day, the Carusos load up the loaner car and head out for rustic Stony Pines, a fairly undeveloped stretch of open plains and rocky crags looking down on the pounding surf of Long Island Sound, which separates New York from Connecticut.

Their ten-year-old house is a four-bedroom, three-bath extended log cabin built on stilts. It sports a wraparound deck and has a fairly steep plank stairway in the front. It is surrounded by a forest of pine trees. It's the perfect secluded getaway spot. Everyone is excited as they head for the Long Island Expressway.

No one notices the dark-colored car following them.

CHAPTER SIX

The family getaway is serving its purpose as the shortened family begins to recover its somewhat forgotten sense of togetherness. During their rather brief stay, they eat all of their meals as a family and watch television together on dad's latest toy, a fifty-inch high-definition wall-mounted television set. They even play some board games together, although it is a bit difficult to get dad to sit still long enough to play "kid" games with Carmella and C. C. Harmony is the byword for their sojourn.

C. C. is particularly enjoying their special family time, except when her thoughts wander to Fluffy, her pet cat. She really misses seeing Fluffy and feeling her soft fur brushing past her ankles.

Fluffy is an outdoor cat that can come and go as she wishes through a special flap panel in their kitchen door. C. C. didn't get a chance to say good-bye to Fluffy before they left because the cat was out gallivanting about that morning. Even though C. C.'s mom has left out bowls of food and water for the beloved Fluffy, C. C. can't help worrying about her pet's welfare while they are away.

C. C.'s ninth birthday is coming up soon after they return home. Her mother has arranged for a real special birthday party at a nearby Chuck E. Cheese's, a real favorite with C. C.'s age group. There will be pizza, ice cream, a personalized birthday cake, and lots of games. And C. C. can invite as many of her friends as she wishes. C. C. can hardly wait. Her anticipation is mounting.

Friday afternoon, the family packs up again and heads back to Harborport.

Arriving home, C. C. runs through the house looking for Fluffy, to no avail. Mom consoles her, "She's probably running around the neighborhood. She'll be back as soon as she sees our car in the driveway."

Once Carmella gets her house settled, she glances out of her porch window to assess the appearance of her flower garden. She is very pleased to find everything apparently in good order. All's well in Carmella's world right now. Mentally, Carmella schedules a full day of TLC for her nursery next week.

Charles checks their mailbox; it is jammed with almost a week's worth of mail including several birthday cards for C. C. The grandparents never miss either of their grandchildren's birthdays. Their enclosed checks are always welcome—and anticipated.

~

While reviewing his lecture notes in the faculty lounge, Professor Anderson is handed a note by one of the attendants. It is from one of his summer students who is requesting a brief meeting with him. Professor Anderson reluctantly agrees and the student is ushered in.

The student starts, "Thank you, Professor Anderson, for seeing me. I'll only take up a few minutes of your time. I'm Greg Thurber. I'm a student in your Toxicology 101 class. I flunked that course in the spring semester. Here's the deal. I'm a starting safety on our varsity football team. I must pass this course to maintain my football scholarship and stay in school."

"I need your help," he continues. "Not to blindly pass me but to counsel me through the course so that I will get a passing grade. I promise you I'll be attentive and complete all class assignments."

Greg concludes nervously with an offer to do any kind of clerical assist for the professor or to run any kind of errand for him; he does have a panel truck on campus.

Professor Anderson's initial reaction to Thurber's plea was abhorrence; how could he be so arrogant? But on further reflection, he respects Thurber's initiative and dedication and accepts his proposition.

Professor Anderson concludes with "I'll be proud to guide you through this course." They shake hands and Thurber leaves the lounge, smiling.

~

At the Sunnyvale dining room, Jonathan finishes breakfast and prepares for another off-campus adventure. He boards the shuttle and heads for downtown Milton, a distance of about fifteen miles. He asks the driver to let him off at the north end of town.

Once afoot, he heads for a garage/office building with a sign reading Acme Limo Services. Several weeks earlier, Jonathan had made arrangements with Anthony Marcone, the owner of the service, to have his son, Willie, drive him around for a day on a per-mile basis plus tip. He doesn't want a limousine, just a regular car. He wants to sit up front with Willie in the car so they can chat as they travel.

Jonathan had called Acme Limo yesterday to set up today's reservation. Willie and his car were prepared for Jonathan.

With his newfound off-campus freedom, Jonathan has developed a growing desire to get out and explore the world around him.

Today he wants to drive by Yankee Stadium in the Bronx and Shea Stadium in Queens. The newspapers are always full of stories and pictures of the Yankees and the Mets baseball teams and where they play. Now he will get a chance to actually see both stadia before they are replaced with new ones.

As he and Willie head off on their mission, Jonathan is amazed at the network of interchanging highways and the number of cars on them. "Wow," he says to Willy, "I never imagined it to be like this."

Just as he is absorbing the wonder of the highway system, they come upon the George Washington Bridge. Its sheer magnitude shocks him. And when he looks down at the Hudson River, seemingly miles below, he shivers with excitement.

Just over the GW Bridge, they head south on the Henry Hudson Parkway, which will take them to Yankee Stadium. Soon they can see its statuesque silhouette. Jonathan is taken aback by the sheer size of it.

Once over yet another massive bridge, the Whitestone Bridge, they are nearing their second destination. Just off the Long Island Expressway stands Shea Stadium. While impressive, it pales in comparison with Yankee Stadium.

The boys stop at a fast food drive-in and enjoy a couple of double hamburgers and Cokes before heading back to Milton.

They arrive back at Acme Limo in late afternoon. Jonathan is so pleased by the tour and Willie that he includes an extra tip for him on top of the agreed-upon fees. Feeling quite proud of himself, Jonathan heads off with a jaunty step to catch the return shuttle to Sunnyvale.

~

The big day has arrived; Mother and the birthday girl start out for the twenty-five-minute drive to Hempstead. Most of C. C.'s friends have accepted her invitation to celebrate her ninth birthday at Chuck E. Cheese's, a real favorite among young children. C. C. can hardly contain her excitement.

Chuck E. Cheese's is all set for her party. A special room has been readied. A special hostess greets C. C. and her mom as they arrive. Happy Birthday C. C. signs and banners bedeck the room. When all of her friends arrive, they are served pizzas and sodas. Afterward, they are given tokens to play the many games that are available. This will be a birthday party that will long be remembered by C. C. and her friends.

When it is time for the birthday cake, the candles are lit and everyone joins in singing "Happy Birthday to C. C." C. C. blows out the candles. She closes her eyes and secretly wishes to see her precious cat Fluffy again. The cake is sliced and passed out to each of the girls along with ice cream and more soda. The mood is electrifying. It is finally time to open the many gifts.

One by one, C. C.'s friends present their birthday cards and gifts to her. C. C. opens each card and reads it aloud. She can hardly believe the many thoughtful gifts she is receiving.

When the last girl presents her gift, C. C.'s mother notices that there is one gift left unopened. She notes that the card is computer generated and is addressed to Cara, not C. C. "Hmm," she wonders. Nonetheless, she hands the present to C. C.

C. C. reads the greeting: "Happy Birthday, Cara. Wish I was there with you. Enjoy your present, Erin."

C. C. is so excited about her big day and all the gifts she has received that she reads the card's message without catching what it said. In her joyful mood, she tears off the wrapping paper and opens the box. Wrapped in multicolored tissue paper lies her precious Fluffy. But Fluffy isn't purring. And her beautiful bejeweled collar is missing.

C. C. screams and drops the box and card. She faints to the floor. Her mother rushes to pick her up and hold her in her arms. "Oh my God," she screams, "who could have done such a terrible thing?"

The staff at Chuck E. Cheese's hears the commotion and rush in with wet compresses for C. C.'s forehead and neck while Carmella pats her hands. C. C. is quickly revived and cradled in her mother's arms.

The rest of the guests are visibly shaken and rush to their parents for support and an exit from this terrible scene.

Carmella braces herself and telephones Charles. She explains the situation as best she could. Charles tells her to stay put; he will be there as fast as he can. He can hardly believe what he just heard. "Who could have done such a vile act?" he muses.

Charles calls Coco Crandel, his PI, on his car phone while driving to Hempstead. He tells Coco what he knows to this point. A thorough investigation must be started immediately. Coco agrees to meet Charles at the Chuck E. Cheese's in Hempstead as soon as possible.

Coco is already there when Charles arrives. Carmella bursts into tears when she sees Charles and rushes into his arms. "Oh, Charles," she murmurs, "how could someone do this to our baby?" "I don't know," responds Charles, "but I'll be damned if I'll stop until we find out."

Coco gets right down to business. He starts by interrogating the store manager. "How do you think this package got into the present stack? Do people often drop gifts off for a birthday party?"

The manager explains that occasionally, people do drop off presents. Coco asks who could have accepted such a package earlier today. The manager calls in two of his assistants and asks if either had accepted a drop-off present today. One of the young men, Jimmie Dolan, says that he did accept a package around ten o'clock that morning. His recollection of the deliverer is that he was a white boy in his midteens and about five feet six.

Coco presses him for more information. Jimmie adds that the kid was wearing a New York Yankees baseball cap. He had it on backward. He was also wearing a Polo jacket with a logo on the chest. Coco thanks him and gives him one of his PI business cards in case he thinks of anything else or if he sees the kid again.

Coco puts on a pair of sterile vinyl gloves and carefully places the box with Fluffy in a black trash bag. He will deliver them to a forensic investigator that he has worked with over the years. The package will be checked for fingerprints, and Fluffy's body will be examined to determine the cause of death.

Coco also places the birthday-greetings envelope and card into a plastic sleeve. He will have them also checked for prints. Then he will have the font and imprint analyzed to see if they can determine what brand and model of computer was used.

Coco advises Charles and Carmella that he will stay on top of this case and will keep them posted.

The Carusos both leave for home; C. C. rides with her mother.

~

Thursday morning, Irene drives up to Sunnyvale to pick Jonathan up for their jaunt over to Long Island and the Carusos' homestead. Following her GPS directions, Irene heads north toward the fabled seaside village of Sands Point with its multimillion dollar estates. A few more miles farther along the coastline, they see the Welcome to the Quaint Village of Harborport sign overhead. A few more turns and they come to Soundview Estates, the Carusos' gated community.

Irene drives up to the gatehouse in the guest lane. The guard asks their business. Irene responds that she and her husband are considering the purchase of the Caruso house on Starfish Lane and he would like to drive by it and view it. She assures the guard they will be in and out in no time. The guard asks for their names and is advised that it's Mr. and Mrs. Anderson.

The guard notices several other "guest" cars are now waiting in line to get into the community, so he speeds up their clearance process. The guard merely records the Anderson name and the property owner being visited as Caruso in his daily logbook. Then he opens the gate and waves them through.

They find Starfish Lane and locate the Carusos' house. Jonathan almost can't believe the size of the house and the beautiful colorful nursery at its right side.

Irene pulls into the driveway and parks her car. She asks Jonathan to go up to the front door and ask Mrs. Caruso if they can visit her flower garden. She will meet him over on the other side of the house in the garden. Jonathan gladly follows Irene's suggestion. No one answers the front doorbell, so he walks past the three garage doors over to the garden. Irene has just finished her tour of the garden and meets him at the gate. Together they walk over to the car and leave.

Jonathan notices that Irene seems a bit shaken by the experience but doesn't say anything. And she has a handbag over her right shoulder.

Jonathan can't decide if he is pleased for the Carusos and their good fortune or resentful of their callowness. *How did they raise their son to cause such human suffering?* he wonders.

~

Sue receives a call from a nurse at Columbus Presbyterian Hospital and is told that her husband has taken a severe turn for the worst. She suggests that Sue come to the hospital as soon as possible.

Sue immediately calls Irene and asks her to accompany her for support. She is expecting the unthinkable. Irene agrees, and to save time, they decide where to meet.

When Sue and Irene arrive at the hospital, they go directly to Dan's room.

They enter his room only to find a white sheet draped over Dan's head. "God help me," shrieks Sue, "he's already left me."

A nurse comes rushing in and says, "I'm so sorry you were not conditioned for his death. He passed on about thirty minutes ago. He was very calm at the end. It was almost like he was at peace and welcomed the hereafter."

Sue is delirious and keeps uttering, "I can't believe it. Dan's gone. I've lost him."

Irene attempts to comfort her but to no avail. Sue can't seem to overcome her grief.

A nurse finally brings in an Ativan tablet and a glass of water for Sue. "Try this, it will soothe your nerves," says the nurse. Sue takes it, and it does have a calming effect on her.

After a few hours, Sue is somewhat composed and asks Irene if she could spend the night at her house. "Of course," responds Irene, "I insist."

CHAPTER SEVEN

"Well, well, look what happened. I wonder how the Carusos are handling their recent family loss. It hardly compares with the Anderson family's grief when their little girl ended up in a coma in a lonely ICU because of that Caruso boy's recklessness. In this life, you have to pay the piper."

~

Coco meets with his forensic expert to review his findings regarding the birthday card, the gift package wrapping, and of course, the Carusos' pet cat.

The birthday card and its envelope revealed numerous fingerprint smudges but none that were discernible. The gift-box wrapping paper provided two sets of crisp, clean prints. One was identified as belonging to Jimmie Dolan, one of Chuck E. Cheese's assistant managers. Coco immediately hoped that one of the others would belong to the package deliverer. Unfortunately, identification of either print could be made because their fingerprints had never been entered in the national computer fingerprint base.

Coco decides to speak with Jimmie Dolan again. He's the key to identifying the identity of the phantom deliverer.

Coco returns to Chuck E. Cheese's again, this time accompanied by a sketch artist. They meet with Jimmie in his manager's office.

Coco starts out, "Jimmie, we need you to help us further identify that kid who delivered the birthday present. You're the only one who got a decent close-up look at him. I need you to work with my sketch artist in coming up with a composite image of him. Armed with this sketch, we'll have a much better shot at locating him."

Jimmie readily agrees. He and the artist work for over an hour, and they accomplish their goal. They present Coco with a line drawing of the delivery person. He looks to be about sixteen years of age.

Armed with the sketch, Coco is encouraged. He starts his search by asking himself where he might find a local boy of sixteen during early afternoon on a weekday. His first thought is to visit nearby Hempstead High School.

Upon entering the school, Coco is stopped by a security guard. Coco introduces himself, explains his mission, and asks to be directed to the principal's office. After hearing Coco's story, the principal calls for all his junior class teachers not presently teaching to come to his office. Within minutes, five teachers arrive. Once there, Coco shows them his sketch artist's rendering and asks if the sketch character looks familiar. Two of the teachers immediately identify the person as Ralph Peters, a junior at the school. Coco feels like he is on the verge of cracking this case wide open but soon discovers that his optimism is misplaced.

Ralph Peters is an honor student and the starting point guard on the school's varsity basketball team. The principal calls him to his office.

Under questioning, Ralph readily admits he did deliver the birthday gift to Chuck E. Cheese's earlier in the day of the party.

Ralph said he was walking past Chuck E. Cheese's when a person in a car at the curb called him over and offered him twenty dollars if he would just drop off a package at the restaurant for him. He said that the party was a surprise for some little girl and he didn't want to chance blowing it.

Ralph thought the request was legitimate enough and twenty dollars is twenty dollars. He agreed and took the package into Chuck E. Cheese's.

Coco pressed him further on the appearance and mannerisms of the man. Aside from remembering the fedora with the brim turned down and the raincoat with the collar turned up, all he could recall was a somewhat husky voice.

Ralph also thought that the car was an ordinary-looking sedan, possibly a Ford. And it was either black or dark blue.

~

Coco returns to his office to prepare a formal report detailing the results of his investigation so far for submission to Charles Caruso. He includes the analysis from the computer technology firm that studied the print on the birthday card to determine the brand and model of the computer used to prepare it. They have determined that the computer used was an Apple Mac Pro with a PenzeSerif 1.0 font.

This computer model is part of Apple's Education Assistance Program, which provides Apple computers to qualifying high schools and colleges throughout the United States and Canada at substantial savings.

Coco recounts how he contacted the Apple Corporation in California to determine the distribution pattern of these educational computers in the New York / New Jersey markets. The Apple Corporation was very amenable to helping authorities curb criminal activities where their products may be involved.

Their Education Assistance Program computer-distribution records indicate that eighty-six Apple MacPro computers were purchased by Strafford College over the past eighteen months. None were purchased by Hempstead High School.

Coco notes in his report that there is no way to positively identify the specific user or computer involved in the preparation of the birthday card.

Separately, he presents his veterinarian's findings on the cause of death of Fluffy. He determined that Fluffy had been suffocated.

~

Meanwhile, Sue has made arrangements for Dan's funeral services. Dan had often expressed his desire for cremation when and if. Sue will honor his last wishes.

There will be an open-casket viewing in the nave of St. Martha's Church, followed by a funeral Mass offered for Dan's eternal soul. After the Mass, the funeral director will transport Dan's body to the crematorium.

Irene and Randolph support Sue throughout the funeral service. A number of Sue and Dan's old friends and neighbors attend and console Sue. Together they help Sue get through this day of a thousand hours and agonies.

~

Jonathan plans his next exciting road trip. He would like to drive out to Long Island again but this time to visit the headquarters of Caruso

Construction Company. He is enthralled by the questionable doings of the Caruso family. Jonathan hops on the Sunnyvale jitney bus and heads for downtown Milton. And then on to Acme Limo. Willie is waiting. Jonathan hands Willie their destination address, and the new adventure begins.

Shortly after noon, they arrive at the impressive headquarters of Caruso Construction Company. It's a three-story structure enhanced by striking stucco-sculptured detailing and two massive red front doors. Mounted along the roof line are the gleaming silver letters that spell out Caruso Construction Company.

Willie drives around the building to its large parking lot. There they notice several uniformed young men identified with the logo for King of Oil over their chest pockets and on the backs of their black coveralls.

There is a black panel truck that further identifies their services as On the Spot Oil Changes and Car Washes.

With his interest in automobiles and their care, Willie stops his car and gets out to talk to one of the men. He finds out that they only service cars owned by their commercial clients and their employees throughout Suffolk County on a scheduled date each month. Caruso Construction Company's service date is the second Tuesday each month. Owners of cars requiring service must identify the services requested to the company's receptionist. King of Oil bills the company each month for all services rendered.

Willie is fascinated with this service and takes notes. His father back at Acme Limo will be very interested in this venture and its potential.

Willie hops back into his car and excitedly explains the program to Jonathan.

As they exit the Caruso Company's parking lot, Jonathan notices several vacant parking spaces in the front of the lot closest to the building. He asks Willie to slow down so he can read the names on the reserved posts. Jonathan reads two of the names out loud, "Charles Caruso and Bruce Byrnes."

Satisfied with their visit, they head for the Long Island Expressway and home base.

~

The next day, Irene calls Jonathan at Sunnyvale to arrange for her next visit with him. She gets through to him quickly. He is very pleased to hear from her again. It seems to Irene that he wasn't sure she would call again. Irene reassures him and asks if her best friend can join them for their get-together.

"As long as it's not your husband," jokes Jonathan. Irene replies, "No worry on that score; he's not even close to being any kind of a friend of mine after what he caused poor Erin."

Jonathan gleefully agrees. They set the date and time and bid each other good-bye.

CHAPTER EIGHT

On one of her free days during the week, Irene travels to the Easton General Hospital. She approaches the main reception desk and introduces herself to the petite blue-haired lady manning the post. Irene then asks to see Dr. Edwards.

The receptionist pages Dr. Edwards, and he responds. She explains that Erin Anderson's mother would like to talk with him for a few minutes.

In barely no time, Dr. Edwards comes walking over to them from the bank of elevators. He smiles as he recognizes Irene.

"How are you doing, Mrs. Anderson?"

Irene responds, "I'm okay. More importantly, how is Erin doing, Dr. Edwards?"

"Unfortunately, there's no new developments, which is a bit of a blessing. Erin is still comatose. I can't really say much more at this time. I'm sorry."

Irene thanks him for taking a few minutes to speak with her. She shakes his hand, smiles weakly, and leaves the hospital.

~

For the next few weeks following the embarrassing conclusion to the meeting at his father's office with Donald Langsford concerning his DUI case, Chip Caruso has resisted making contact with his father by avoiding the family evening meal. He arrives home each night an hour or so after his father's normal bedtime. This whole matter upsets Carmella, Chip's mother.

She insists on knowing the cause of this father/son rift. Well into the second week of Chip's family dinner boycott, Charles finally explains how weird Chip acted during their meeting with their attorney, Donald Langsford.

Charles continues, "I really don't know what his problem is. Here we're putting together the best possible defense for him and his DUI charge. The goal is to protect him from being found guilty and losing his license. He might even be facing jail time. And all I get from him is a sense of indignation. Against what, I don't know. He was the one who drank to excess that day and was involved in that terrible accident that caused serious brain damage to a young girl."

Charles concludes with a request to his wife, "When you see him tomorrow morning, please tell him to drive out to my office anytime tomorrow after one o'clock. I'll have a face-to-face talk with him and get to the bottom of this." Carmella agrees.

At just after two o'clock, Chip arrives at his father's office and is announced. His father invites him to sit down in one of the upholstered chairs in front of his desk. He joins him in a facing twin chair.

Charles begins, "So what's your problem? And why the attitude?"

Chip doesn't respond at once but finally snaps back, "When I graduated from college, I thought you wanted me to join your company in an executive position. It's almost two months and here I am, angry and without a job. That's what it's all about."

Charles is taken aback with Chip's grievance and responds, "That was my original plan, but when I heard about your drinking habits and your DUI, I thought maybe you have some growing up to do before you join the family business."

Chip quickly replies, "Fine, forget about me. I'll get my own job. And my own apartment. You won't have to deal with me."

Charles is flustered by Chip's belligerence. "Let's not make this into a family feud."

Chip hops up from his chair and adds, "Okay. Let's just go our separate ways." He leaves.

~

With his disappointing meeting with his father behind him, Chip moves on to plan B—get a new address and a good job. First, the job. He begins responding to executive recruitment advertisements in the Sunday editions of the *New York Times* newspaper.

The job offerings from National Products Corporation and Broadscope Communications interest Chip the most. He contacts both companies and arranges interviews with representatives of each company in New York City hotel suites.

The first interview is with Broadscope, a national communications and cable company. They are seeking recent college graduates with engaging personalities to join their cable television advertising sales teams. They presently have openings in their Braintree, Massachusetts and Columbia, Maryland offices.

The other company, National Products Corporation (NPC), manufactures and distributes branded paper products nationally. They are seeking energetic young go-getters in their metro New York City region. The position entails sales/merchandising to chain supermarkets and drugstores. Their openings are in Bergen County, New Jersey; Rockland County, New York; and Suffolk County, New York.

After interviewing with both companies, Chip decides to pursue a career with NPC if he can be assured of securing the Suffolk County, Long Island territory.

The Human Resources Manager for National Products offers Chip his preferred territory. He is scheduled to attend their introduction to NPR marketing course at their Flushing office in Queens, New York. His starting salary and bonus arrangement are agreed upon. An added benefit is a Chevrolet Equinox Crossover, all expenses paid.

Chip shakes hands on the offer; he will start the first of next month. He is so proud of himself in landing this great position with a quality company.

~

Sue heads to a centrally located diner to meet Irene for lunch. They discuss the many events of the past week.

With her involvement in her new job as a customer representative for a major corporation, Irene is more at peace with the world than Sue.

Sue still can't accept the fact that her great friend and husband are gone from her life forever. Irene comforts her and offers to pick her up at her apartment for their next MADD meeting. While Sue's anguish was not totally caused by some drunken driver, she still feels guilty for her involvement in this drunken-driving disaster.

Irene agrees, and they arrange to go to the meeting.

~

C. C. is so excited. Her Dad is taking her over to the town's pet shop this weekend. While it is almost impossible to replace her old Fluffy, Dad has convinced her to accept another young Siamese cat and make her a part of their family.

Come Saturday, Dad and C. C. drive over to the pet shop. C. C. is a bit apprehensive, but when she sees the large selection of beautiful cats, she relaxes and quickly decides that she does want another Siamese cat.

One of the caged cats seems to be returning C. C.'s glances and meowing. "That's the one, Dad," says C. C.

An accommodating salesgirl notices C. C.'s excitement and lifts the cat from her enclosure and hands it to C. C. to hold. That clinches the sale. Dad heads to the checkout counter and completes the sale for their new Siamese cat. He also purchases a beautiful collar, a litter box, and a bag of litter.

The three of them head home while C. C. is dreaming up names for her new furry friend. She finally settles on the name Muffy, and Dad agrees.

Once home, C. C. introduces Muffy to her mother and then shows her around the house, including the location of the litter box. Unlike Fluffy, Muffy will be an indoor cat. C. C. is not going to take any chances this time. To guarantee that, Dad screws shut the flap panel in their kitchen door.

~

Professor Anderson receives a page to report to the dean's office as soon as possible. The mother of one of his students is on the phone in a frantic mode. Her daughter, Catherine Mulholland, has come down with a severe case of the flu and is bedridden.

Mrs. Mulholland continues, "She left her textbooks and class notes for your Toxicology 101 course in her locker." She adds, "Could I impose on you to have someone unlock her locker and retrieve them? If you could have them packed up and shipped collect overnight by UPS, I'd really appreciate it."

Mrs. Mulholland further explains that Catherine is scheduled to graduate this year and needs that course credit. Without the course materials, Catherine will fall behind her classmates.

Feeling magnanimous that morning, Professor Anderson agrees to package all the materials and get them out to Catherine overnight. Her mother provides Professor Anderson with their nearby Long Beach address and thanks the professor for his thoughtfulness. "Catherine will make both of us very proud," she concludes and hangs up.

~

Professor Anderson recalls his football student's offer to run some errands for him with his truck in return for favorable consideration during his course.

The professor arranges for one of the resident janitors to unlock Catherine's locker for a moment so he can extract the materials that Mrs. Mulholland mentioned. He packs them in a box, seals it, and addresses it.

After class that afternoon, he asks Greg Thurber to stay a few minutes. "What is it professor?" he asks. "Is there a problem?" Professor Anderson assures him he is doing fine and adds, "I need you to perform a mission of mercy. One of your fellow classmates, Catherine Mulholland, has come down with the flu and can't attend classes for a while."

Professor Anderson continues, "Her mother called me and asked if I could pack up her course materials and arrange for their delivery to her house in Long Beach on the south shore. It's about a thirty-minute drive. Do you think you could drive over there this weekend and deliver this package?" Greg jumps at the opportunity. "I'd be glad to." The professor shakes his hand and slips him a twice-folded hundred-dollar bill. Greg takes the package and the bill and leaves with a wide grin.

~

Irene calls Jonathan at Sunnyvale and arranges for a return visit with him. He is very excited about the thought of seeing her again and talking with her.

In an effort to provide Jonathan with a little insight into his twin brother's interests and professional doings, Irene enters Randolph's study and surveys his desk. She notices the five textbooks for his summer courses and that they are set aside, as if having been read and previewed. She also notices a second set of the same books, so she feels comfortable taking the "used" books.

Irene picks up Sue on her way, and together they're off to Sunnyvale. Upon arrival, Irene introduces Sue to Jonathan and then presents Randolph's books to him. Jonathan is quite pleased with Irene's gesture. He promises to read each of them cover to cover. Irene is tickled and suggests, "Maybe someday you and Randy can get together and discuss them."

"No way, Irene," responds Jonathan. "We crossed that bridge a long time ago."

Irene switches subjects and asks Jonathan, "Do you ever envision a world in which you and your brother could meet and talk with each other?"

"That will never happen. I'll never forgive him for what he did to me," spurts Jonathan.

Irene continues on the same track and asks Jonathan, "Do you remember anything about your brother way back when you both were eight?" She adds, "Was he a good brother before the accident?"

Jonathan thinks for a moment and responds, "He was always aggressive and self-centered. He wasn't nice to me. I basically just tolerated him."

With Irene making such strides to befriend him, Jonathan decides to open up a bit on his recent exploits. He explains about his new off-campus time setup. Jonathan reveals the arrangement he has made with a local limo car service. Using this service over the last few weeks, he reveals that he and Willie, the limo company owner's son, drove out to the Caruso Corporate Headquarters on Long Island.

Jonathan then describes his drive around Mr. Caruso's corporate headquarters building including that unusual oil change and car wash service that was operating in their parking lot while Jonathan was there. Jonathan remarks, "Willie, my driver, was so excited about this on-site service that he took all sorts of notes to bring back to his father."

Irene thanks Jonathan once again for taking the time to see Sue and her, "I'll see you again real soon. Maybe one of these days, I could pick you up with my car and we could spend the whole day together." Jonathan sheepishly grins. Irene and Sue rise, shake hands with Jonathan, and leave.

On their way to Sue's apartment, Irene broaches the subject of Sue moving into Irene's home. Sue initially rejects the kind offer, saying she would be intruding on her and Randolph. Irene assures her that she would not be intruding; they have a spare bedroom that she could use. Irene continues, "It would benefit both of us as we deal with our issues. Think about it. You don't have to make a decision right this minute." Sue agrees to seriously consider such a move.

~

While walking down to pick up her mail at curbside, Carmella spots a neighbor, Patricia Holms, walking her dog and says, "Hi, Pat, how are you?"

Pat responds, "I'm fine, Carmella, but did you hear about Janet?"

Janet is Pat's next-door neighbor. Shocked, Carmella answers, "No, what about her?"

Pat explains, "She was rushed to the hospital yesterday. She had flulike symptoms, but the doctors aren't sure her problem is really the flu. She's undergoing tests to try and figure out what's making her so sick."

Carmella asks, "What hospital is she in? I want to visit her and see how she's doing." "I believe she's in Long Island Central Hospital," replies Pat.

When Carmella gets to the hospital, she finds out that Janet is in Room 412W from the registration desk personnel. She rushes up to the fourth floor and heads for Janet's room. As she enters the room, she is shocked at what she sees. Janet's complexion has taken on a light bluish hue. And she is receiving oxygen through a nasal respirator.

Janet's husband, John, is sitting at her bedside, holding her motionless hand. Janet is semicomatose with IV drips connected to her arms, providing her with necessary nutriments and saline supplements. Her temperature, pulse, and blood pressure are all being monitored.

Carmella speaks, "Gosh, John, how did all this happen? Was she sick?"

"No," replies John. "She was fine until a couple of days ago. Then without warning, she started to run a fever and throwing up. Soon her breathing became so labored that I rushed her to the hospital. The doctors at first thought it was some strand of influenza. But now, they're not so sure. They are calling in pulmonary specialists to review all the data and to examine Janet. I'm concerned because her condition is still deteriorating in spite of their efforts to help her."

Carmella tries to reassure him, "She'll pull through, John. Our prayers are all with her. And she's strong and has always taken good care of herself."

While Carmella is with Janet, John takes advantage of Carmella's presence and excuses himself. He leaves Janet's room and walks up and down the halls trying to clear his head and fathom the complexity of his wife's condition and, worse yet, her prognosis.

John returns to Janet's room and thanks Carmella for her concern and support. She grasps his hands and squeezes them and says, "If there is anything my family or I can do for you and your family while you're here in the hospital, please let me know. In the meanwhile, know that we will all be praying for Janet and you." John nods his head silently. Carmella promises to return tomorrow, hugs John, and departs.

~

As Carmella heads back to Harborport, she ponders Janet's quagmire. What could possibly have caused her medical maelstrom? Why isn't she responding more rapidly to the doctors' interventions? And, perhaps more importantly from a personal standpoint, what about her own flulike symptoms? Carmella had not mentioned them to John, but she herself had similar symptoms a few days ago but to a much-lesser degree. Her head is spinning from these unanswered questions.

At around two o'clock in the afternoon the next day, Carmella receives a phone call from Pat Holms.

Pat begins, "Hello, Carmella, I'm sorry to be the bearer of bad news, but Janet passed away around noontime today. The hospital classified her cause of death as uncertain since her symptoms went far beyond those of the flu. I'll keep you apprised of her funeral arrangements as soon as I know them. Talk to you soon. Bye."

Carmella wonders, *Could my garden be the missing link in Janet's death? It seems like the only common location I can think of that both of us visited. I'll have to investigate that connection a lot closer.* Then she adds, *I think I'll stay out of the garden until I resolve some very serious issues. In fact, I'll lock up the nursery to keep everyone out as well.*

~

Since the cause of Janet's death could not be ascertained by the hospital staff, by law it must be reported to the Nassau County medical examiner for determination on the need for an autopsy.

The medical examiner, Dr. Ralph Naismith, reviews the hospital's records and decides a forensic autopsy would be required in this case.

CHAPTER NINE

Professor Anderson is well into his summer teaching sessions. Both of his courses have enrollments of twenty-five to thirty students. Most of the students are alert and responsive. There are the ones who are taking the courses for the first time. There are, however, five or six students in each course who visibly demonstrate why they failed the courses the first time around.

While Professor Anderson tries to ignore the antics and attitudes of these malcontents and underachievers, he firmly believes that their very presence minimizes his ability to effectively present his courses to the other deserving students.

Professor Anderson's frustration level peaks. Fearing that his temper is about to erupt, he chooses instead to cancel the rest of his afternoon classes. Classes will resume tomorrow.

With idle time available, Randolph gets in his car and drives aimlessly out to the general location of the Caruso Construction Company. That's the company owned by that bastard kid's father. That should help him clear his brain or not.

As Randolph ponders the events of the past few months, he suddenly wonders what lies ahead for him and Irene and their marriage. He can feel her animosity toward him ever increasing while she drifts apart from him. It seems to Randolph that Irene and Sue are developing a bond far stronger than his marriage bond with Irene. And Sue is not as friendly to him as she once was. The future seems quite murky.

~

Donald Langsford's administrative assistant contacts ADA Tangradi's office to determine the status of the two motions that they submitted back in early June. He is advised that ADA Tangradi is prepared to schedule a pretrial conference to review the current charges and possible pleas.

With several phone calls, the pretrial conference is scheduled for Thursday of next week at ten o'clock in ADA Tangradi's conference room.

At the appointed time, Donald Langsford, Charles Caruso, and Chip Caruso arrive and are escorted into the designated conference room. They take seats at an elegant, twelve-foot-long mahogany conference table.

After introductions, ADA Tangradi opens the proceedings with "We have thoroughly reviewed all elements of this case including your well-prepared briefs in support of your motions."

Tangradi asks Langsford to orally present his motions. Donald graciously accepts the offer and introduces their first motion to suppress the results of the flawed BAT machine results due to the police department's failure to have the particular unit calibrated on schedule as required by the manufacturer. With no other tests to substantiate the DUI charge against Charles Caruso Jr., he respectfully asks that the DUI charge be dismissed.

As a follow-up to that motion, he also requests that the secondary felony charge of reckless driving causing serious injury be amended to a misdemeanor charge of simple reckless driving. This request seems reasonable in light of the dismissal of the DUI charge and the fact that no fatalities were caused by the accident.

Donald concludes with "An independent accident investigatory company, experts in the field, affixed 68 percent of the culpability for this accident to the other driver. A major factor in this rating was the fact that Mrs. Anderson, the other car's driver, was totally distracted by a cell phone call she took right before the accident. She actually ran a red light at the impact intersection. We trust that your office will concur with our findings and rule accordingly."

ADA Tangradi thanks Donald Langsford for his fine presentation and turns to Chip and asks, "Well, young man, what have you got to say for yourself?"

Chip, caught unaware, meekly responds, "Sir, I'm incredibly regretful for my part in this terrible accident. I promise to amend my ways and act more responsibly from here on out."

Tangradi nods affirmatively and adds, "I do hope you have learned a valuable life lesson. That being said, I now wish to discuss pleas and penalties to resolve this case."

Donald quickly responds, "Thank you for your valued consideration. My client here is prepared to plead guilty to a misdemeanor charge of reckless driving. In light of that plea, we would offer our recommendations on the appropriate penalties. We would recommend a $2,000 fine, a ninety-day restriction on his driver's license to daytime hours, which will allow Charles Jr. to pursue his professional career, his enrollment in the DVD's alcohol, education, and prevention program, and finally, a one-year probation period."

ADA Tangradi replies, "Your assessments and ours are almost in sync. We are recommending a $3,000 fine. We can accept your modification of the ninety-day driver's license suspension. Can we all shake on these amendments?"

Quickly, Donald agrees after getting affirming nods from Charles and Chip and extends his hand to Tangradi, "Thank you sincerely for your forbearance and reasonableness in this case."

Tangradi adds, "We will set a date to present our agreement and pleadings to Judge Johnson and inform your office."

Everyone stands and leaves the conference room.

Three days later, the same assembly stands before the honorable judge Roger K. O'Neill. After the amended charges are read, Charles Caruso Jr. pleads guilty as charged. The court accepts his plea and imposes the agreed upon penalties.

~

Having obtained a guilty plea to the amended charges from one of the parties involved in the May automobile accident, the DA's office decides to also amend Irene Anderson's charge of felony reckless driving to a misdemeanor.

~

Youth Escapes DUI Charge with Plea Bargain
Child Victim Remains in Coma in ICU

This headline in the local paper tells it all. The accompanying article identifies the "lucky" driver who beat the DUI rap as Charles Caruso Jr., son of scion Charles Caruso of Harborport, Long Island. The piece goes on to explain the terms of the plea bargain—a reduced charge of reckless driving, a $3,000 fine, one year's probation, and a ninety-day limited restriction on his driver's license. The eight-year-old girl Erin Anderson, who was severely injured in the accident, remains in a coma in the ICU at Easton General Hospital.

~

Later that week, Irene and Randolph are summoned to come to the hospital as soon as possible. They rush to the hospital and are soon sitting bedside with Erin. Nurse Edmonds details Erin's worsening condition and assures them that she will be with them throughout the day.

Several hours later, the Andersons are startled by a drone sound coming from Erin's heart monitor, indicating a lack of cardiac activity. Nurse Edmonds rushes into the room and immediately calls in a Code Blue, a high-urgency call to designated doctors and nurses to respond at once. Within minutes, two specialist doctors and three ICU nurses rush into the room. The lead doctor orders an epinephrine injection for Erin while the other doctor applies electrical shock pads to her tiny chest in an attempt to restart her heart.

Time seems to stand still. And then what seemed incomprehensible only a few short days ago actually happens; Erin is pronounced dead at 11:23 AM.

~

Throughout the evening news that day, the local cable TV newscasts report the "breaking news" of Erin's passing. Their reporting includes a recap of the accident details as well as the deal that Chip Caruso got from the DA's office.

One of the broadcasts featured a remote transmission from in front of the exquisite Caruso home in Harborport, Long Island. The local reporter had plenty of commentary including a reference to the loss of a beautiful young bloom like Erin while the camera crew panned across Mrs. Caruso's colorful garden.

~

Irene briefly discusses her plans for Erin's burial with Randolph; he agrees with them. Irene contacts a local funeral home and arranges for Erin's viewing and funeral. She will bring over Erin's favorite dress for the viewing. The one-day viewing will be held the day after tomorrow, followed by a funeral mass at their family church, St. Martha's, the next morning. At the conclusion of the church service, the funeral director will lead the cortege to the Holy Cross Cemetery in Woodview.

~

"The way our judicial system administers justice is totally lopsided. The young girl has paid the ultimate price for that kid's negligence, and he gets off with a slap on his wrist. What lesson will other young drunks learn from this? Simply that they can act irresponsibly and still avoid the full weight of the law—if they have the right lawyers and a rich and connected father. Charles Caruso Jr. recklessly took the life of that precious little angel, yet he is free to cause even more heartbreak and sorrow. It's just not fair. Someone should do something about him before he has another 'accident'."

~

The Andersons handle the three-hour viewing at the funeral home as well as could be expected. Many of Erin's elementary-school friends show up to pay their respects. Mrs. Duffy and several of Erin's friends from the dance academy are also among the first to arrive.

Irene has her face buried in a handkerchief most of the time, trying to hold back a cascade of tears. This is not the way life is supposed to play out. It is excruciatingly painful for a mother to say good-bye to her only child and love.

The cemetery service is even more emotional for both Irene and Randolph as they watch the pallbearers carry Erin's little casket to her final resting place. Father Hernandez of St. Martha's Church leads the assembled in parting prayers for Erin as her casket is lowered into the grave. Irene breaks down, crying. Randolph puts his arm around her shoulders and attempts to console her. Most of the group come over to them and offer their condolences again and move out.

~

As Randolph surveys the crowd, he thinks he recognizes a somewhat familiar figure, but who? After intense concentration, he finally hones in on the face that he had seen on television the other night. It's that Caruso kid.

Randolph leaves Irene's side and rushes over to confront his little girls' killer. As he approaches the Caruso kid, Randolph thrusts forth his arms toward the kid's chest. Chip is stunned and falls over. Randolph stands over him and shouts, "Murderer, you killed my daughter!" The young man mumbles an almost inaudible "I'm sorry." Randolph damns him and in a loud voice utters, "I'll kill you." Other members of the funeral party are shocked at Randolph's explosive outburst and rush to separate the two combatants. Once they're separated, the funeral party all head for their cars and leave the cemetery.

~

Irene invites Sue Greene to sit with her at a private memorial luncheon she and Randolph arranged for a few of their close friends and relatives.

During the luncheon, Sue leans over to Irene and says, "Every day, I thank the good Lord for our long friendship, especially now that we are both dealing with such personal tragedies. Together, I believe we can get past today's hardships." Irene's eyes well up as she acknowledges Sue's declaration. "Thank you, thank you, and thank you. You are indeed a great friend. I know I couldn't have survived these terrible days without you at my side."

CHAPTER TEN

Professor Anderson is presenting his last summer session before final exams. As is his wont at the end of each course, Professor Anderson performs a self-critique of his performance in the areas of preparation, delivery, and student comprehension. In all three categories, he honestly rates himself well above average; such superior evaluations encourage him to match or top them in subsequent courses.

Professor Anderson is particularly gratified by the stellar performance of his special student project this summer. Footballer Greg Thurber not only is completing his course with a perfect attendance record but is earning a B+ for the course, subject to his final exam result. And Greg achieved this above-average performance without the granting of any professional favors. Greg fulfilled his part of their arrangement set earlier in the course. He was the consummate student, and he did run several errands for Professor Anderson with his truck.

~

The final session of Applied Toxicology 101 deals with Green Toxicology, the issues associated with toxic elements in the residential environs. The students are surprised to learn about the many toxic elements in and around their homes. Professor Anderson directs his students' special attention to pages 289–312 in their Green Toxicology textbook by Professor Boehme. There they find much discussion of the numerous toxic components often found in residential settings, both indoors and outdoors.

Many of the indoor contaminants, such as lead, radon, and carbon monoxide are familiar to the students. On the other hand, everyone is surprised by the number of poisonous plants found in residential settings. Of the most poisonous (oleander, water hemlock, rosary pea, deadly nightshade, and castor bean), several are known to the students. To stimulate the class, Professor Anderson shows them several of the most toxic plants including the rosary pea plant and the water hemlock plant.

"As you can see, the rosary pea or *Abrus precatorius* has very attractive seeds. Most of the rosary pea seed is a bright red color, and the smaller portion of the seed is a jet-black color. The rosary pea seed is quite hard and is harmless to humans and animals. Only when the coating is scratched or damaged is the poisonous seed powder released in a potent state. Here's a sealed packet of the toxic powder from the rosary pea plant. As you can see, it looks harmless, like ground pepper."

Professor Anderson continues, "Another deadly plant is this water hemlock plant. Notice the pretty purple-striped leaves and its small white blossoms. Ingesting one of these leaves will do you in in short order. Anyone want to try a bite?"

He concludes with "Remember the old adage, 'You can't tell a book by its cover.' It's particularly true when it comes to these deadly but alluring killers."

~

With his summer-school schedule rapidly drawing to a conclusion, Randolph Anderson decides now would be a good time to put a call into the office of Dr. Ramon Stevenson, his long-term counselor and psychologist, and set up an appointment. Randolph has a myriad of personal issues to discuss with the good doctor. At the foremost is his relationship with his wife since the car accident and the death of their only child, Erin.

Having set an appointment to see Dr. Stevenson, Randolph experiences an intense feeling of positivism in taking this first giant step in resolving his and Irene's mutual issues and hopefully to preserve their marriage.

Randolph arrives at Dr. Stevenson's office on schedule. Their counseling session begins with the doctor asking Randolph what he would like to accomplish in today's session. Randolph explains the circumstances that lead up to his daughter's painful death and the subsequent blame game that followed. The doctor is busy taking notes and nodding.

When Randolph completes his representation of the events from his standpoint, Dr. Stevenson announces that he will now assume what he perceives as Randolph's wife's mental and emotional state. In this assumed state, he will ask Randolph some directed questions. He tells Randolph that he will probe the real motives behind his behavior that fateful evening and possibly help him understand and accept his wife's stances. Dr. Stevenson advises Randolph to lie back, close his eyes, and let the words flow freely from his mouth.

The doctor begins, "Remember, these are your wife's questions. Answer them openly, not defensively."

"Question number 1: what was so consuming on campus that night that you forgot to pick up our daughter after her dance lesson? Question number 2: why didn't you go and pick up your daughter immediately after receiving my phone call?"

Randolph ponders both questions for a while and decides to fess up to the truth. He begins, "Actually there was no faculty meeting that evening. It was a faculty poker game. I got all caught up in the excitement of the game and totally forgot about my daughter's pickup."

He goes on, "When my wife called, I was in the middle of a huge winning streak. It was the only night all year when I was winning consistently. I just couldn't quit at that point, so I lied about the faculty meeting running late."

"Randolph, I admire your candor. We're making real progress," states the doctor.

Dr. Stevenson continues, "Can you understand that your wife has been asking herself those very same questions over the past few months? They are the basis for her blame game with you. I believe that your wife blames you to mitigate her own feelings of guilt in causing the accident."

Dr. Stevenson begins his session summary with a call for mutual openness, "The truth will out. To make progress in your relationship arena, both of you have to be honest with each other. It's the first step you and your wife have to take to mend your damaged relationship. Trust will follow. I suggest you discuss all this with your wife in a pleasant surrounding away from your home—perhaps her favorite intimate restaurant. And remember, no more accusations, just the bold, bare facts."

Randolph shakes hands with Dr. Stevenson and thanks him for his valued advice and insight.

Randolph is imbued with a renewed sense of understanding and forbearance as a result of his lengthy session with Dr. Stevenson. He decides to follow the doctor's recommendation and fess up to his wife about his activities on the night of the accident and admit his partial culpability in the accident that hospitalized their daughter.

He informs Irene that he just completed his consultation with his psychologist, Dr. Stevenson. He says that the doctor was most helpful in sorting out his role in the car accident. As a result, Randolph would like to share his newfound understanding with her. To accomplish this, he has planned a special catered dinner for just the two of them this coming Friday evening when Irene returns home from her day in the field. Hesitatingly, Irene agrees to Randolph's apparently sincere proposal.

Friday evening happens and Irene arrives home and is welcomed by Randolph and a dining room table beautifully adorned with fresh flowers and lighted candles. Irene heads upstairs to shower and primp for their formal dinner.

When Irene joins Randolph at the dinner table, they agree to hold off their discussions until after dinner so as not to diminish the enjoyment of the meal and the ambiance.

Roger, their tuxedoed server for the evening, presents Irene with a bottle of Robert Mondavi Chardonnay, her favorite wine, for her perusal. With her nod, Roger uncorks the bottle and pours a sample sip for her evaluation. Irene sips and approves; Roger pours Irene a glass.

Randolph prefers Coppola Cabernet Sauvignon. Roger presents a bottle and performs the same uncorking and sampling before serving Randolph a glass.

Randolph raises his glass and proposes a toast to the evening ahead, "Here's to a productive evening." They clink glasses and sip.

Course after course is served meticulously with innate class by Roger. When they complete their scrumptious meal, Roger clears the table and serves Irene and Randolph their favorite after-dinner drink, Crème de Menthe in distinctive snifters. They take their glasses and move into the study for the evening's discussion.

Randolph begins, "Dr. Stevenson suggested that the old bromide 'honesty is the best policy' still reigns supreme in relational interactions. I've thought long and hard about what he said, and I agree. I want to clear my conscience once and for all and bare my soul about the accident. The night of the accident, I wasn't attending a lengthy faculty meeting. I was playing poker with several of my fellow professors. I forgot all about picking up Erin after her dance lesson. And to make matters worse, I could have left when you called. I didn't because I was on a winning streak, which I didn't want to break."

Randolph continues, "I hope you can see a way to forgive me for my horrible failures. I'm not sure I'll ever get past them myself, but you're a better and bigger person than I am. Can you ever forgive me?" Randolph asks pleadingly.

Irene doesn't utter a sound at first but then opens with "You bastard! I somehow knew all along that you were fabricating your version of that evening. No, I can't forgive you for ruining my baby's life. It will remain with me until I die. I'll never be able to see you other than as the kidnapper of my daughter. You stole her from me."

Randolph foolishly attempts to mitigate his complicity in the accident scenario, "How about your distracted driving that night? Maybe if you weren't on your damn cell phone you could have avoided the collision altogether."

His rebuttal and fury only serve to steel Irene's disgust for him.

Irene rises and stares right at Randolph. With a weepy, halting voice, she speaks, "We're finished. This can't go on. I want a divorce from you. It's the only way I can go on living."

Irene stomps out of the study and heads for her bedroom upstairs. She slams the door closed after entering and then locks it. Her wailing resonates throughout the house. It's hours before she finally lapses into a soporific state.

~

Irene wakes the next morning, tired and troubled. What a horrible evening last night was. On the other hand, she senses a modicum of smug satisfaction in finally discovering the truth about Randolph's activities and attitude on the night of that tragic automobile accident.

Irene decides then and there to contact a divorce lawyer and initiate divorce proceedings. She still can't believe she was such a bad judge of character in choosing Randolph as her mate and father of her daughter.

After her usual morning eye-opener, a hot cup of black coffee, her mind begins to stabilize. She decides to call Sue Greene and fill her in on last night's doings. Irene calls Sue and makes plans with her for dinner that evening. Sue will drive over and pick her up at six o'clock.

~

Hours later, Sue pulls her car into Irene's driveway and instantly notices something most unusual. Both of Irene's garage doors have several concrete blocks set on the rubber weather stripping running along the base of the doors, obstructing the automatic operation of the doors.

Alarmed at what she sees and what it portends, Sue hops out of her car and pushes the blocks off the weather stripping. She can't open either door since she doesn't know their electronic entry code numbers.

Sue runs to the front door and rings the bell. When she receives no response, she heads for the side garage door. It's not locked, so she enters the garage.

Irene is slumped over her car's steering wheel. Sue rushes over to the side garage door and instinctively pushes the button controls mounted to her right side near the doorjamb. Both overhead doors spring into action and open in unison.

Sue opens Irene's car door; she is conscious but very groggy. Sue helps her exit the car and stumble out of the garage to her side lawn and an ornamental iron bench. Irene sits down and begins rapid breathing.

"Carbon monoxide poisoning," Sue beams. "You were almost killed. Who could have placed those concrete blocks on the doors' rubber molding to disable your automatic garage doors?"

Irene is rapidly regaining total consciousness. She responds, "I wanted to drive over to Fast Mart for a quart of milk before you got here. I remember it was about a quarter to six when I got into my car. I started the engine and activated my door control in the car to open the garage door. I sure am lucky that you arrived on time. Another few minutes and I would have been a goner. I owe you my life."

Sue asks, "How could this happen? Someone deliberately placed those heavy blocks on your garage door weather stripping."

Irene responds, "Randolph would be the likeliest suspect. We had a real blowout last night. We are now so far apart that divorce is our only remaining option."

Sue replies, "I'm sorry to hear that. But do you really think he would attempt to kill you?"

"If not him, then who?" answers Irene.

"In any case," continues Sue, "you should report this threat to your life to your local police department and have them investigate it."

Irene agrees, and they get into Sue's car for a short ride to a favorite haunt of theirs.

CHAPTER ELEVEN

Randolph is furious. His well-thought-out plan of reconciliation exploded into hurtful shards of rejection and anger. He decides that he has had enough. He's getting out. As soon as possible, he will pick up his belongings and move out. And he'll get even with Irene for her nastiness.

Randolph returns to his campus and visits the college's housing office for some advice on available apartments off-campus. The staff provides him with several options including a two-bedroom house within walking distance of the campus.

The house is an easy choice. It is nestled between two stately colonial-style houses and shares their well-manicured landscape appearance. Randolph contacts the owner of the house, and they agree on a reasonable lease and monthly rent.

Once Randolph is the rightful lessee of the house, he braces himself and calls Irene. After exchanging brief hellos, he informs her that he will be coming by this Saturday to pick up his bedroom set including the two bureaus and the bedroom's area rug. He will also move out all of his clothes and shoes from his closet. And finally, he will clear out his study, including his computer and printer, and his workbench and cabinet.

Irene feels that Randolph's requests are surprisingly reasonable and promptly but curtly agrees, "See you first thing Saturday." "Okay," responds Randolph, and he hangs up.

Randolph places a call to his student comrade, Greg Thurber, to solicit his help this coming Saturday morning. He explains that he and his wife are divorcing and he's moving into a rental house near the campus.

Greg quickly agrees to help out. He is very pleased to be developing a relationship with the professor. Professor Anderson is highly thought of around the campus.

~

C. C. prepares for Halloween and her favorite fall activity, trick or treating. This year, she is going to be "Alice in Wonderland." Her mother has purchased a beautiful costume for her, and C. C. is most happy. As a personal safety precaution, C. C. and her parents have agreed on some basic ground rules for this year. All trick or treating will be done during bright daylight hours and only within the confines of their gated community. C. C. agrees not to talk to any strangers no matter how appealing their Halloween offering might be. And there will be no solo trick or treating; C. C. must be accompanied by at least two of her neighborhood friends or schoolmates. Already neighbors, Katie and Mo (short for Maureen) have signed on and will join C. C. for Halloween trick or treating. She can hardly wait to get out there in her spectacular costume.

It's four o'clock, and the girls are decked out in their striking costumes and excited to get going. They head out of C. C.'s house after a chorus of good wishes from C. C.'s mother. House after house, they are greeted by friendly, happy neighbors pleased to see them. Compliments abound as do the treats.

Hours roll by, and the trio is having a fabulous time. They already have lots of candy, favors, and fun memories. They have just about covered the entire community. Their timing is perfect. Nightfall will be upon them soon.

There is only one house left to visit. It's at the end of a broad cul-de-sac. This house is not adorned with Halloween decorations like most of the other houses in the community.

Katie speaks up, "Maybe we should skip this house. It has a For Sale sign on the front lawn. There's probably no one home anyway."

Mo, the spark plug, counters, "Don't be silly, there's a car in the driveway. C'mon, let's do it!"

C. C. concurs, "Katie, don't be such a scaredy-cat."

The trio walks up to the entranceway hand in hand, with trepidation.

As they approach the front door, it flies open, and a huge Frankenstein-like monster lurches toward them and groans menacingly. The monster beckons them to enter.

C. C., Katie, and Mo, as if on cue, scream and race back down the front walk. They never stop running until they get to C. C.'s house.

C. C.'s mother hears the commotion and rushes down from upstairs to find out what's up. Excitedly they explain the cause of their alarm. Mrs. Caruso is relieved to discover their horror is the result of an adult prankster who enjoys scaring the hearts out of young children. She reassures the girls while making a mental note to check out the occupants of that for-sale property.

~

Chip Caruso is also preparing for some Halloween activity of his own. He's invited his longtime buddies, Johnnie Tegins and Pierce Redmond, to join him for a Halloween bash at his parents' summerhouse in Stony Pines. It's no doubt his last stay at their vacation home for a while.

Promises of thick juicy steaks, lots of cold beer, and a sleepover seal the deal; and Johnnie and Pierce sign on.

The three buddies meet at Chip's parents' house at six o'clock on Halloween Saturday. The beer, steaks, baked potatoes, and corn on the cob are packed in ice in a supersized picnic cooler and set in Chip's company car. By seven o'clock, they're well along the way to Stony Pines.

Once underway, Chip asks the guys if they have room for a third roommate at their newly leased house in Rego Park. Enthusiastically, Johnnie and Pierce each respond with a positive yes. Chip explains what led up to his decision to move out of his parents' home. They agree on next Saturday as the move date. Johnnie will drive his new panel truck out to carry Chip's larger furniture items.

It's still twilight time when they arrive at the Carusos' summer retreat. The guys are surprised at what they see. Apparently, the house has been visited by some Halloween pranksters the night before.

The house and the surrounding trees and shrubs were "teepeed." Toilet paper rolls had been thrown into the air at the house and surroundings. The toilet paper streamed down like a cascade of white water over falls. It was a real mess.

Then they noticed a major crack in the front picture window of the house and realize it's a lot more than a prank situation.

Chip unlocks the front door and all three enter the great room. They immediately notice the large sprayed-on black-paint message across the screen of the new giant television screen—Fat Cat. Johnnie puts his arms out and cautions his pals, "We should call the cops before we disturb any evidence." All three agree, and Chip calls the Stony Point Police Department and reports the vandalism. The dispatcher informs Chip that she will send a patrol car unit to his house to view and document the vandalism.

The patrol car arrives within fifteen minutes, and Officer Tim Farnan steps out and identifies himself. He opens his log binder and begins his official report. Chip points out the cracked front window and the defaced television screen. Officer Farnan makes a note of each and takes out a digital camera and photographs both.

Chip asks if it would be all right if his friends go outside and begin removing the toilet paper from the trees and shrubs. Officer Farnan approves as long as they don't touch anything else. Then he and Chip begin a tour of the interior of the house. As they enter the spacious kitchen, they notice a large puddle of water below an opened freezer door. Officer Farnan cautions Chip to stay out of the kitchen so they don't disturb any evidence.

Toward the middle of the kitchen, Officer Farnan makes note of the partially opened kitchen door. One of the door's small glass panels had been smashed. The shards are scattered around the door. "Apparently, that's how they got into the house," remarks Farnan. He places the shards in a plastic evidence bag.

As they exit the house, Chip comments, "I thought it was just a Halloween prank when we first drove up to the house. When we got out of our car, I noticed the cracked window. And when we went inside, there was the ugly spray on the television screen. That's when we called for help."

Officer Farnan completes his notes and advises Chip, "Our detective squad will look into this matter. They will probably contact you on your cell phone first thing tomorrow morning and arrange to come out to visit the scene. Stay out of the great room and the kitchen until they get here." He packs up and leaves.

Chip calls home to fill his parents in on what's transpired at Stony Pines. His mother answers his call, and when Chip starts to tell of the vandalism, she cuts him short and says, "Hold on, let me put your father on to hear this."

His father picks up the line and says, "What happened?" Chip fills him in on what occurred at the house. "I called the Stony Point Police Department and they sent an officer out. He took pictures and wrote up a report. He also said that a detective will come over tomorrow morning to begin an investigation of the entire matter."

His father is seething and asks, "Who the hell could have done such a nasty thing?"

Chip answers, “Damned if I know. Someone seems to have the Carusos in their crosshairs. I'll call if I find out anything else.” He hangs up.

Chip calls his buddies, Johnnie and Pierce, away from their cleanup mission to get the planned cookout and party going. They fill the fire pit built into the front deck with firewood and set the fire. Soon they have a roaring fire going. The steaks, aluminum-wrapped ears of corn, and baking potatoes are strategically arranged on the huge circular grill. Chip breaks out the well-chilled beer and the much-delayed party is on.

Soon the happy trio is enjoying the fine food and beverages under a clear crisp starless Long Island evening. Around midnight, the festivities come to a halt. The group tidy up the area and hit the sack. Tomorrow will be a busy day.

Just after ten o'clock the next morning, Chip hears his cell phone ring. Upon answering it, he's informed that two Stony Pines detectives will be arriving at his house in about ten minutes. He jumps into action, waking his comrades and encouraging their participation in the new day. The front doorbell sounds and Chip opens the door and comes face-to-face with Detectives Ryan Kuhn and his assistant, Kieran Lavin. Both police officers present their badges and introduce themselves to Chip and his associates.

Detective Kuhn begins, “We're here to investigate the break-in and vandalism you reported. We'll be taking many pictures as well as videos. But before we begin, we want to fingerprint each of you to eliminate your prints from the others that we uncover. Let's take care of that chore first. Chip, will you lead off?”

Detective Lavin opens his fingerprint kit and proceeds to “print” the three current occupants. He then leaves the group to dust other pertinent elements of the premises for prints.

Detective Kuhn, using a high fidelity voice recorder / video camera, interviews each of the young men and notes their observations about the previous twenty-four hours.

Since Detective Kuhn had noted a blood smear on one of the kitchen door panels that Detective Farnan had collected the day before, he decides to also obtain a DNA sample from each of the young men.

By one o'clock in the afternoon, the detectives wrap up their investigation and are ready to return to the police station with their collected evidence.

Detective Kuhn thanks them all for their cooperation and hands each one of his cards, in case something else strikes them. He and Detective Lavin depart.

CHAPTER TWELVE

"Well, the stakes seem to be rising. I guess you just can't shirk the responsibility for your irresponsible actions. The Carusos are surely paying for the sins of their son. As the good book preaches, 'An eye for an eye and a tooth for a tooth.' So be it."

~

Bruce Byrnes, Caruso Construction's vice president of Municipal Bidding and Contracting, enters Charles Caruso's office. Bruce is there to update Charles regarding the status of their current municipal bidding progress.

Using a printed chart on a tripod, Bruce reviews the company's outstanding bid submissions:

PROJECT	CARUSO BID	UNSEALING DATE
Roslyn Public Library	$18.25 MM	Oct. 10
Millville Administration Bldg.	$20.46 MM	Oct. 12
Roselle High School Addition	$ 9.41 MM	Oct.12
Nassau County Auditorium	$22.71 MM	Oct.15
Freeport Pier Restoration	$16.89 MM	Oct. 16

Caruso Construction relies on a steady flow of municipal contracts. Year in and year out, such contracts account for 55 to 60 percent of the company's total dollar volume. Through their experience with the municipal bidding process and their constant contact and follow-up with the bidding agencies, Caruso Construction can count on being granted most of the projects on which they have submitted a bid proposal.

Bruce comments, "Word around the island is that we have a new competitor bidding on each of these projects. And they could grab several of them from us. But not from underbidding us. Let me explain. The new company is the Granite Construction Company out of Brooklyn. They are apparently well financed and should have no difficulty in posting any required construction bonds."

"To make matters even worse, they claim to be a certified minority-owned company. The principal owner of the company is Mrs. Rosa Bianco as in the Bianco Crime Family."

Charles responds to Bruce's report, "I don't mind a little competition; we can compete with the best of them. But I'm concerned with their claim of minority ownership and management. That really gives them a leg up on us in the municipal bidding process."

"We've got to dig into this company's corporate structure and background. If we can prove that one, they are mob controlled or two, they are not really a true minority-owned and operated organization, we can dismiss them as serious contenders."

Charles continues, "Contact our law firm and have them probe into this company and discover the true facts about them. Our law firm, Langsford and Reynolds, has enough influential contacts at the state level in Albany to uncover the facts. And make sure you inform them of the urgency of this matter so they put the project on the front burner."

"I'm on it," responds Bruce as he packs up his materials and departs.

As soon as Bruce leaves his office, Charles places a call to Coco.

"I've got another job for you," Charles begins. "We have a new competitor, Granite Construction Company, out of Brooklyn. They claim to be a minority-owned enterprise. And that's the rub. Being minority owned and operated gives them a distinct advantage in bidding on municipal construction projects, our bread and butter. They claim their minority status is due to the company being owned and managed exclusively by Mrs. Rosa Bianco. That's right. She is the wife of mobster Tony Bianco."

Charles continues, "What I need you to do is enlist several of your retired ex-buddies from the New York City Police Department and tail Mrs. B. day and night for thirty days. I need to know if she really does manage Granite Construction or if it's all a giant sham. I'll get you her home address as well as the company headquarters' address. Can you handle this kind of assignment?"

Coco replies, "Its right up our alley. I know exactly who I am going to call for this job. We'll get on this within a few days."

Coco contacts Jack Greenley and Matt Penza, two of his most-trusted and reliable ex-buddies on the New York Police Department. They are both retired from the force. They all agree on a date and time to meet to discuss an interesting proposition at the Mid-Island Diner in Garden City.

Coco welcomes Jack and Matt and explains the assignment. They are to stake out Mrs. Bianco at her home in the Beach Haven section of Brooklyn and follow her whenever she travels from her home during the hours between six o'clock in the morning and six o'clock in the evening, seven days a week.

Coco provides them with a five-by-seven-inch color photograph of Mrs. Bianco as well as a black-and-white aerial print of the Bianco's three-acre walled estate. He points out that there is only one entrance/exit through the steel gates on the north side of the estate. There is a manned guardhouse at the gates.

Coco provides them with a GPS tracking device for attachment to Mrs. Bianco's automobile as well as a portable receiver for their car. They will have to devise a plan for planting the magnetic device on her car.

Finally, Coco instructs them to rent a drab, nondescript sedan for their stakeout.

The group exchanges thoughts and ideas and finalizes their plan of action. The stakeout begins in two days and runs for a total of thirty days, including weekends. They agree on a per diem rate plus expenses. They shake hands and leave the diner to get ready for their adventure.

The first two weeks of their stakeout are uneventful. Mrs. Bianco ventures out of her walled sanctuary only a half dozen times. Twice she goes to the Church of the Resurrection to attend Sunday Mass. It is in the church's parking lot that they are able to attach the GPS transmitter under her car.

Three other excursions take her to the nearby Waldbaum's Supermarket for grocery shopping. The only other departure is for a visit to her dentist's office. That was it. No visits to the Granite Construction Company's headquarters during the two-week period.

As Jack and Matt drive into the Bianco's neighborhood to begin their third week of surveillance, they locate an ideal parking space with an unobstructed view of the Bianco's guardhouse.

It's Matt's turn to walk back up the street to Marie's Luncheonette to pick up their usual morning fare—two coffees and two apple strudels.

Marie's has a self-service coffee station with four to five types of coffee from regular to decaffeinated. Matt fills two coffee cups and caps them. He snaps a handy cardboard tray into shape and lodges the coffee cups into the configured openings. He places the small cream cuplets and the apple strudels in the flat middle portion of the tray.

As Matt heads back toward their car, the sun is about ready to rise and shine. The overhead streetlights have dimmed. Holding his coffee tray with both hands, he walks past an alleyway on his right side between two apartment buildings. He doesn't notice the two husky figures lurking in the shadows.

Both thugs are upon him before he knows it. One strikes the back of his legs at knee height with a metal pipe. Matt drops his tray and falls forward as the other goon hits him behind his right ear with a leather-covered black jack rendering him semiconscious.

They drag his limp body into the alleyway and start kicking him all over while demanding to know "who you work for?"

Not receiving a response from their groggy victim, they frisk him and steal his pistol and wallet while leaving the GPS transmitter from Mrs. Bianco's car as their calling card. Checking for any witnesses and seeing none, they slink out of the alleyway and head down the street.

When Matt doesn't return within a reasonable period of time, Jack's natural detective suspicions are aroused. He exits the car and heads back toward the luncheonette. About halfway there, he spots the spilled coffee cups and the tray lying on the sidewalk near an alleyway. He now knows something's afoul. He draws his service pistol and carefully edges into the alleyway. He soon catches sight of a leg protruding from behind several trash cans. He rushes over and finds his partner lying there, moaning. And beside him lies the GPS transmitter.

Matt starts regaining consciousness as Jack strokes his hands. Jack advises him to stay put while he goes back for their car. Jack rushes back to their car and pulls out of their parking space. He hurriedly backs up the street in reverse to the alleyway and double parks.

Jack helps Matt up and together they stumble to their car. Jack slides Matt into the car. He calls 911 for the location of the nearest hospital. They head off for Beach Haven General Hospital.

Matt is admitted for observation. A preliminary exam by a triage nurse surmises that he has suffered a mild concussion and several broken ribs. Jack calls Coco and fills him in on what has transpired.

"Obviously," Coco begins, "they're on to us. We'll have to abort our surveillance mission. Return the rental car in the meantime. I'll follow up on Matt's condition and notify his wife. I'll get back to you when the dust settles."

~

The administrative offices of Long Island Central Hospital receive a registered mail from the Nassau County Medical Examiner's office. It contains the official results of the autopsy performed on the body of Janet Zook.

The standard autopsy confirmed the hospital staff's findings of "no unusual wounds, contusions or other life-threatening factors" observed. Based on the suspicion of an internal mechanism as the cause of death, the coroner proceeded with a forensic autopsy to pinpoint the cause of death.

Employing a gas chromograph in conjunction with a mass spectrometer, portions of Janet Zook's body tissues were studied and analyzed.

The conclusive findings of this analysis are that the patient's cause of death was attributed to the inhalation of abrin, a poisonous substance.

Since there is no knowledge at this time as to the source of this poisonous substance, the medical examiner has referred this case to the Nassau County District Attorney's office for investigation.

~

Irene decides to investigate the procedures to follow, to obtain a divorce in New York State. She "googles" the subject on her computer and is amazed at the wealth of information available online.

Irene is particularly pleased to discover that she and Randolph can obtain a legal divorce in New York State without engaging the high-priced services of lawyers.

To qualify for New York's version of a no-fault divorce, spouses have to live apart from each other for at least a year before a divorce can be filed.

Also, both parties must execute a Separation Agreement, which must be filed with the Nassau County Clerk's office before the one-year period begins to run. The Separation Agreement details the financial division of all the assets of the parties as well as any spousal support involved.

Irene calls the Nassau County Clerk's office and asks for the forms clerk. Once connected, Irene asks the clerk if she would be kind enough to fax her two copies of a blank Separation Agreement. The clerk agrees to do so. Irene provides her fax number, thanks her, and hangs up.

She then attempts to itemize all of her and Randolph's assets as well as their liabilities. Her plan is to keep the house and credit Randolph with his net portion of the house. Her final balance sheet was about equal for both parties. Irene is going to prepare a document outlining the divorce procedures as well as the accounting division of their net worth. She will also fill out a Separation Agreement form for Randolph to review and hopefully sign.

Irene will also propose the granting of monthly spousal support in the amount of half of the monthly mortgage payment including local property and school taxes plus two thousand dollars per month as long as she remains unmarried.

Irene will provide Randolph a copy of this document on Saturday morning in a sealed envelope. He can take it back to his quarters and review it by himself. When he has had time to absorb the information and its ramifications, they can get together and finalize the division of their assets and the amount of spousal support. Irene will then submit both her and Randolph's signed Separation Agreements to the County Clerk's office for filing.

Irene double checks Randolph's bedroom and closets to be sure everything is ready for the movers. She notices that several of the large cardboard boxes and the jumbo zippered plastic storage bags that Randolph had dropped off at the house for the move were not fully packed and sealed. She accumulates Randolph's remaining items and puts them in the plastic bags by category; she then packs the bags into the extra cardboard boxes and securely tapes them.

CHAPTER THIRTEEN

The Nassau County District Attorney's office assigns Robert J. Thompson, PE, a chemical engineer under contract with the county, to investigate the unusual death of Janet Zook. His assignment is broad based, covering the purchase and placement of the poisonous substance as well as uncovering the perpetrator of the crime.

Thompson's first step is to visit with Janet Zook's family and to determine her habits and lifestyle. He places a call to John Zook, Janet's husband, and arranges for a visit to their home.

At the Zook house, Thompson offers his condolences and then reviews her final days. He asks if she did anything out of the ordinary during that period. John Zook does recall Janet caring for their neighbor Carmella Caruso's garden while the Carusos were away for a few days. Knowing how much Carmella enjoyed her garden, Janet lovingly pulled out any weeds that popped up in the garden.

John Zook also shows Thompson around their property including their enclosed backyard. While viewing Janet's tomato garden, he explains, "Each year Janet would plant a dozen or so tomato plants. She kept them in an enclosure covered with chicken wire to thwart the entry of rabbits or other four-legged intruders."

John continues, "She kept all of her gardening tools and supplies in her gardening workbench in our garage." Thompson surveys the workbench and finds nothing but the usual gardening paraphernalia. No surprises here.

Before leaving the Zook home, Thompson inquires about the neighbors who were friendly to Janet. John provides Thompson with their full names, addresses, and phone numbers.

Thompson's first call is to Patricia Holms. He explains the purpose of his call and visit. She agrees to speak with him if he can be at her house in the next ten minutes. She has to leave for a doctor's appointment at that time. Thompson agrees and rushes over to her house.

Pat Holmes greets him at her front door. He again mentions his role in the investigation of Janet Zook's death and asks if she has any interest in plants. Pat explains that, unlike Janet, she has no desire to grow plants or vegetables. Her only concession to the horticultural set is the three pots of red geraniums she cultivates each year on her rear patio. Aside from a can of geranium fertilizer, there are no flower garden connections with the Holms' household. Thompson thanks Pat for her cooperation and prepares to move on.

Thompson phones the Caruso house; Carmella answers the call. Once again, George Thompson explains his role in the investigation of Janet Zook's death. He quickly arranges to stop by and see Mrs. Caruso for a few minutes.

Thompson introduces himself and gets right into it. "Janet Zook's autopsy confirmed the cause of her death was her inhalation of the seed of a poisonous berry called the rosary pea. She could have been exposed to this seed in a garden setting. Janet Zook's husband mentioned that she attended to your flower garden a few days before she was admitted to the hospital with flulike symptoms. This poisonous seed produces similar symptoms."

Thompson's presence and sincerity jogs Carmella's memory of her own flulike symptoms after returning from their family's four-day sabbatical to their summer home in Stony Pines. She mentions her mild symptoms to him.

The connection between the two women's symptoms and their time in Carmella's garden leads Thompson to recommend a thorough chemical evaluation of the plants and the soil in her garden. Carmella quickly agrees and Thompson excuses himself to retrieve his hazmat suit and equipment from his minivan. He keeps these items handy for quick on-the-spot evaluations. They protect him from any toxic substances in the garden.

Thompson returns in a few minutes and changes into his hazmat outfit in Carmella's garage. Armed with a supply of sterile sealable plastic bags and a spade, he heads out to the garden.

Before beginning his sampling, Thompson draws a rough layout of the garden with its parallel rows of peonies, irises, and rhododendrons. He then proceeds to sample the soil in each row in ten-foot intervals. He also takes smear wipes from every tenth plant's leaves. All samples are identified and deposited in individually sealed bags for delivery to a toxicology lab near his office in Garden City.

When Thompson completes his sampling effort, he returns to the Caruso garage and spreads out a six-by-six-inch tarpaulin on the garage floor and proceeds to carefully remove his hazmat outfit and equipment and place them in a jumbo sealed bag. Returning to his normal clothing, he packs up all of his bags and sample packs into his car.

Thompson walks up to the Carusos' front door and rings the bell. When Mrs. Caruso opens the door, he thanks her for her thoughtful responses to his inquiries as well as her cooperation. He suggests that she keep everyone, including herself and any pets, from the nursery until he gets back to her with the results from the toxicology lab. Carmella agrees and thanks him sincerely for his help.

Thompson drops the samples and the nursery layout at the lab with the comment that they are looking for evidence of abrin, a most toxic substance and the product of the seed of the rosary pea plant.

~

Saturday dawns and Randolph and his student pal, Greg Thurber, arrive at Randolph's old residence to pick up his furniture, workbench and his belongings.

Irene meets them at the front door with a wintry greeting.

Within a few hours, the men have loaded all of Randolph's wares into Greg's truck and Randolph's Escalade and they are ready to roll.

Irene comes out of the house and says, "Oh, one more thing before you go. Would you ask your helper to lug those four concrete blocks to behind the garage where the other blocks are?"

"No problem," replies Randolph. He asks Greg to move the blocks as Irene requested. In no time the blocks are relocated behind the garage. George wonders these few blocks were left in front of the garage, but he lets it go.

Irene adds, "I want to give you this envelope that we spoke of earlier. Don't open it until you get home. After you have had a chance to digest its contents, we can talk about them."

"Okay," Randolph responds. He and Greg get into their respective vehicles and drive off.

~

Once Randolph and his belongings have departed, Irene decides to drive over to the vet's office and retrieve Erin's pet dog, Alfie. Having Alfie back home again will help restore a feeling of past times around the house. And Irene will enjoy having Alfie sleep in her bedroom every night. Knowing that Alfie is nearby during the night will provide her with a much-needed sense of security.

~

With Randolph and his belongings officially out of the house, Irene decides to call Sue and inform her of the doings that took place that morning. Irene concludes with "Now that Alfie and I will be all alone in this big house, it's time for me to share it with you. C'mon over and join us. We'll have a ball sharing the house, the in-ground pool, and our many thoughts and dreams. What do you say?"

Sue answers, "I've been giving the matter a lot of thought, and now that Randolph is out of the picture, I'd love to accept your kind offer and move in with you."

Irene responds, "Great, plan on moving in at your convenience. It'll be great for both of us."

~

The toxicology lab report is hand-delivered by messenger to Thompson's office. It confirms the presence of abrin, a very toxic poison in the soil of Carmella Caruso's nursery. The lab technician suggests that whoever placed the poison in the soil probably was an amateur. A professional would most likely have only used the toxic powder inside the rosary pea seed. In this case, the perpetrator just mashed the hard-shelled seed to get to the seed dust, which actually is the toxic element. Fragments of the shells were found in the soil. No poison was detected on any of the nursery plants.

On receiving the lab report, Robert Thompson telephones Carmella Caruso and informs her of the toxicology testing. He provides her with the identification of the iris column as being the culprit. He suggests that she contact an environmental services company and have all the soil and plants removed in a safe manner. He adds, "If you don't clean up this toxic area, the county will come along and demand action."

He concludes, "You're a lucky lady to have survived this ordeal. But you have to uncover the fiend behind this evil effort in the first place." Carmella adds, "You're right. We certainly have our work cut out for us."

"Thanks for your help."

~

Charles Caruso receives a registered letter from the Stony Pines Police Department. It is a copy of the department's official record of the vandalism and breaking/entering perpetrated at his family's house in Stony Pines on/before Halloween eve.

The report recites the details of the offenses. Further, it indicates that the three previously unidentified fingerprints found throughout the house have now been ascribed to Mr. and Mrs. Charles Caruso and their daughter Cara.

No discernible shoe prints or tire treads were discovered at the property.

The report was stamped "Open Case" in the status box at the bottom of the form. Beside that entry, the report was signed and dated by Detective Ryan Kuhn.

~

Bruce Byrnes receives his Granite Company minority interest report from Paul Spera, Esq., an associate at Langsford and Reynolds. Research at the Department of Corporations in Albany, New York, indicates that the official corporate filing by Granite Construction Company listed Joseph Bianco as president of the corporation with an 80 percent ownership interest, and his wife, Rosa, as secretary of the corporation with a 20 percent ownership stake.

When informed of their claimed minority ownership with the Division of Minority and Women Business Development (DMWBD), the investigator at the Division of Corporations recognizes the invalidity of Granite Construction Company's minority ownership claim.

The representative of the DofC announces plans to contact DMWBD and inform them of the company's malfeasance. He agrees to also contact the five municipalities with plans to unseal construction bids in the next two weeks.

Bruce proudly presents the good news to Charles Caruso. Charles is impressed with the efficiency and effectiveness of their law firm. Their prompt follow-up with the five noted municipalities should cause the dismissal of Granite's bids and almost assuredly grant each of the bids to Caruso Construction Company.

When Joseph Bianco receives notification that their five bids on Long Island municipal projects were officially rejected due to irregularities in their DMWBD filing, he is apoplectic.

He vows to even the score with that Caruso bunch. And this is a man with a reputation for doing what he says and getting what he wants.

~

Saturday dawns, and Chip finishes his preparations for his big moving day. His father has already headed out to his office. Chip reminds his mother that today's the day. He asks her if it is all right for him to take his bedroom furniture with him. Weepy, she agrees, "Take whatever you want. We won't need it now."

His buddies arrive, and they pack up his car and Johnnie's truck. By noon, they are all set to go. Chip hugs and kisses his mother, and they take off for Rego Park.

CHAPTER FOURTEEN

Robert Thompson calls Carmella Caruso to inform her that he is still investigating the poison-powder case. He needs the Caruso family to sit down together and think long and hard about anyone that might want to cause them harm. Carmella realizes how important this could be and agrees to call a family meeting for tonight right after dinner. She contacts Chip and requests his attendance at this very important meeting. He agrees to be there.

That evening, Carmella waits until C. C. goes to bed and is sound asleep. She then summons the other family members to the living room and explains that they have a mission—they must uncover the names of people who might wish to cause harm to their family.

The family discusses all sorts of angles for well over a half hour but still comes up short. Thinking out loud, Charles muses, "Being in business, I do realize that there are quite a few people who resent my successes. But I can't imagine any one of their resentments rising to the level of violence. The only person I can think of in recent times that would wish harm to us is Joseph Bianco. He's the mafia kingpin that we beat out of a bunch of municipal construction bids. I'm sure he really hated losing those bids to Caruso Construction."

"Even so," Charles continues, "he couldn't be the culprit in the nursery episode since the bids he lost out on were just unsealed this past week. That's a long time after the poison was spread in mother's garden. So we have to rule him out. I guess I haven't been much help here."

Carmella chimes in, “I still can’t think of anyone who hates me or our family enough to try and poison us. I just can’t come up with any names. Sorry.”

Finally Chip gets his turn, “The only person I can think of who could be that hateful is the father of that girl who tragically died as a result of my auto accident back in May.”

When Carmella gets back to Thompson, she passes on Chip’s thoughts. Thompson thanks her and vows to follow up on this promising tip.

Immediately, Thompson contacts the security company under contract with the Carusos’ community for front-gate security and makes an appointment to meet at the gatehouse the next day.

His first step upon arriving at the gatehouse is to introduce himself to the security company’s representative. He then does a visual assessment of the gatehouse and its surroundings. He notes that there are sidewalks on both the entrance and the exit sides of the gatehouse for walking or cycling visitors. These guests can come and go totally unopposed and are not recorded. He wonders who was it that decided that only vehicular-driven guests cause problems in gated communities.

Robert Thompson asks to review the logbooks for the past thirty days and is presented with five three-ring binders. He begins with the earliest date and notes that each guest automobile is listed by (1) date and time, (2) driver or key passenger’s name, (3) purpose of visit, (4) type and make of car, (5) license plate state and number, and (6) the party being visited.

Thompson notices that many entries have limited info with only the date and time, key visitor’s name, and party being visited recorded. He asks the security guard why there are differences in the thoroughness of many of the logbook entries. The guard explains that the community association doesn’t want any vehicle backups at the entrance gate, so the guards sometimes shorten the list of questions and speed up the clearance process.

Thompson proceeds with his review of all the entries, day by day. He is focusing in on the name Randolph Anderson. For the first fifteen days, there’s no sign of the Anderson name. Then on July 16, he notices the names Mr. and Mrs. Anderson cited on the daily log as passengers in a car entering the community. The party being visited was listed as Caruso.

Thompson is pleased to be inching closer to putting this case together. Once back at his office, he proceeds to research the name Anderson through the Internet. He soon discovers that there’s a Randolph Anderson who is a professor of Chemical Engineering at Strafford College on Long Island, New York. His name was in the newspapers in May and June of this year as the father of a daughter, Erin Anderson, who was killed in an automobile accident involving an alleged drunken driver by the name of Charles Caruso Jr.

That's the connection that Thompson was hoping to discover. Now he has to follow up on the source of the abrin poison to see if there is an Anderson connection in the purchase of the poison.

Thompson utilizes the Google and Bing search engines for sources of the rosary pea plant and/or its toxic seed powder.

The searches reveal numerous Asian sources but few domestic ones. The outlets in the United States are concentrated in the northeast portion of Florida. Thompson immediately decides to investigate these sources and calls his contact at the Nassau County District Attorney's office. He fills her in on his progress with the abrin poison case and requests authorization for travel fare to and from Florida plus expenses to research the sources of the poison.

With his record for propriety, Thompson's contact readily approves his request and authorizes their travel department to book his round-trip flight to West Jacksonville Airport.

When he arrives at the West Jacksonville Airport, Thompson rents a car and begins his hunt for the source of the deadly plants that killed Janet Zook.

Armed with a list of eight nurseries or mail-order houses that list the rosary pea plant on the Web sites, he heads out to his first stop at Johnson's Gardens in Fernandina Beach.

He pulls into their parking lot and asks to speak with the owner of the operation. Jim Raschi comes out and introduces himself to Thompson, who presents his ID card and explains his mission of discovery.

Thompson asks, "Does your company sell rosary pea plants or their seeds?" Raschi quickly answers, "We used to, but it was a slow seller, so we dropped it two or three years ago."

Thompson thanks him for his cooperation and departs. He now drives down to the town of Baldwin and eventually locates the Baldwin Fruits and Flowers outlet. Upon arrival, he asks to meet with the owner or manager. The manager, John Mangan, comes out of his office and they introduce themselves.

When Thompson asks if they sell either the rosary pea plant or its seeds, Jackson responds in a positive mode. Thompson then asks if they have a mail-order capability. Jackson answers in the negative, "We only sell retail here at our store. We never ship our goods anywhere."

Thompson then motors over to White Springs Outlet in White Springs.

After being introduced to Ralph Beaton, the owner, Thompson asks if they sell the sought-after plant or seeds. When informed that they do sell that species, he asks if they have a mail-order component. When told that they do ship orders around the country, Thompson asks if they maintain records of those out-of-state sales.

Beaton responds, "We're very remiss in that area of our business. We treat it like a stepchild. Sorry."

Thompson thanks him for taking the time to speak with him and for his frankness. Feeling a little dismayed, he heads off to his next stop.

At Bountiful Acres in Starke, Thompson meets Ken Benson, the manager. After introductions, Thompson asks if Bountiful Acres markets rosary pea or its seeds out of state. Benson confirms that they do ship orders out of state.

Thompson asks if he could review their out-of-state sales records for the past sixty days under a pledge of confidentiality. Benson agrees and provides Thompson with a computer printout of their out-of-state sales and shipments to review.

About halfway through the records, Thompson comes upon his target subject. On June 2, two dozen rosary pea plants and two water hemlock plants were shipped to a Randolph Anderson in New York and charged to his personal MasterCard account.

Thompson asks for and receives a photocopy of the records associated with Randolph Anderson's purchase of rosary pea plants.

Thompson concludes his visit with "Thank you so very much. You may have helped solve a very perplexing homicide case. I'll keep you abreast of our progress as we move forward."

They shake hands and Thompson gets into his car. He heads north toward the West Jacksonville Airport with hopes that he can book an earlier flight back to LaGuardia Airport in Flushing, New York.

~

Columbus Day falls on the second Tuesday of October. It also is the scheduled date for the monthly visit of the oil-change crew to the Caruso Construction Company's rear parking lot to service their employees' cars.

It's a beautiful fall day with temperatures expected to be in the midseventies by afternoon. Charles Caruso decides to take advantage of the fine weather and drive his classy '54 Chevy Impala convertible to work.

While the King of Oil crew are busy servicing a dozen or so cars throughout the wide lot, one of the men notices an apparently male figure in black coveralls and wearing a black peak cap with a wisp of blond hair barely visible around the ears. The unknown figure is carrying several long-armed items which couldn't be readily identified from a distance.

After working for a few minutes underneath one of the up-front cars, the figure leaves the lot.

At a little after six o'clock, Charles Caruso leaves his office and proceeds to the parking lot. There's only a smattering of cars left at that time.

He carefully unhooks his car's convertible cloth top and folds it back into the rear storage well. To complete the classy look, he covers the top with its leather boot and buttons it down securely. He's all set for a smooth, nostalgic cruise home.

Within a few minutes, westward bound, he enters the Southern State Parkway. Most of the evening's rush-hour traffic is home by now, so Charles makes good time. As he approaches his exit, the driver of a car in the middle lane suddenly decides to exit even though he passed the exit ramp. He veers over the triangular safety zone heading into the path of Charles's car. Charles lets out a loud swear and jams on his brakes, to no avail.

Charles is in shock. His brakes are not responding. His beautiful Chevy plows into the rogue car's passenger side. Both cars grind to a halt.

Charles never had seat belts installed in his vintage car and is thrust forward into his steering wheel.

Fortunately, both cars were traveling at reduced ramp speed so the injuries to both parties turned out to be superficial.

Within fifteen minutes, a NY State trooper's patrol car rolls up. He calls for two tow trucks to clear the ramp area. In the meantime, he directs ramp traffic around the impacted cars onto the grassed shoulder.

Charles and the other driver exchange license and insurance information. The trooper takes pictures and completes his accident report.

Charles calls home on his cell phone and arranges for Carmella to pick him up.

~

The next morning, Charles has Carmella drive him over to the tow truck company's lot. He is particularly interested in what caused his brakes to fail.

"Someone cut your brake lines under the car," offers their chief mechanic. "If you like, we can replace the lines when we work on your front-end damage. We should have a firm estimate available for your review later today. Give me your contact information. I'll call you with the estimate number and e-mail you the detailed estimate."

Charles thanks him and joins Carmella for their return trip home. Once home, Charles changes into business attire. Before leaving for his office, he addresses Carmella, "You were asking the other night about people who might want to do us harm. This is another hint. Someone actually sabotaged my car. They cut my brake lines. I was very fortunate that I was going slowly at the time I applied my brakes."

Carmella is teary eyed. Charles hugs her tenderly and whispers, "We'll be all right. I'll get Coco on this right away." He gets into his newly repaired Lexus and sets off for his office.

CHAPTER FIFTEEN

Caruso Company VP Paul Burke has a hectic workweek coming up. Each day of the week, he will be appearing at the official openings of the construction bids in the five municipalities across Long Island where Caruso Construction has submitted sealed bids and performance bonds.

While the municipalities normally do not mandate attendance at these bid unsealings, Caruso Construction has had a long-standing policy of always attending these official events. Having a company officer at the unsealing of the bids guarantees that no last-minute surprises occur.

With Granite Construction's bids being rejected for falsification of official records, Caruso Construction should win all the bids, assuring the company's continued success over the next year.

~

Susan Dapper, executive secretary to Charles Caruso, lets out a scream and yells, "Oh my God!" Everyone turns toward her to see what the matter is. Charles hears the commotion in his office and comes rushing out to Susan's desk at the door to his office.

"What is it?" Charles patiently asks as he reaches Susan's desk. He looks down and sees a partially opened USPS Priority Mail package with what appears to be a fish in a ziplock plastic bag.

While the other secretaries are consoling Susan, Charles opens the package completely and removes the sealed bag. It is indeed a dead fish.

Charles knows that a dead fish is a warning of doom from the Mafia.

Charles checks the shipping label and sees that the package is addressed to him at their headquarters address.

The addressee section is blank except for the shipping point of the sender.

He is shocked to see that the package was sent from his home post office in Harborport, New York.

Charles takes the package and the plastic bag into his office. That seems to have a calming effect on Susan, and she murmurs, "Thanks."

Charles will address this disturbing new issue with Coco as soon as he arrives. He is scheduled to meet with Charles in about an hour to tackle the cut-brake-lines matter.

Irene places a call to Jonathan so that she can arrange for another day on the road with him. Sue won't be accompanying them on this outing. The plan is to pick him up at Sunnyvale Meadows next Tuesday at ten o'clock in the morning.

The two of them will do some sightseeing in nearby Pennsylvania, have a leisurely lunch, and be back at Sunnyvale by four o'clock.

Jonathan is most pleased by Irene's invitation. He quickly accepts and thanks Irene for her kindness. Irene concludes the call with "Great. I'll see you next Tuesday at ten. Bye." Irene is really getting to enjoy her private time with Jonathan.

Coco arrives at the Caruso Construction Company headquarters and is quickly ushered into Charles's office.

"Good afternoon, Charles."

"I'm pleased to see you, Coco. Things are really starting to heat up around here."

Charles leads Coco into a stately oak-paneled conference room. He says, "We can spread things out on the conference table."

"Okay, let's get started, Coco. First off, on Tuesday past, someone cut the brake lines on my '54 Chevy. As I was driving home that evening, some idiot cut in front of me on the exit ramp of the Southern Parkway. I jammed on the brakes only to discover that I had no brakes. I rammed into the other car. Fortunately, we were both going slowly at the time of impact, so neither of us suffered any serious personal injuries. The tow truck operator was the first to discover that my brake lines had been severed. Now we have to find out who the culprit was."

Coco responds, "These guys are really playing for keeps, Charles."

Coco continues, "Obviously the brake line had to be cut in your parking lot since the brakes had to be functioning on your trip from home that morning."

Charles adds, "That's right. The car sat in our rear parking lot all day long. The brake lines had to have been cut sometime during the day in the parking lot."

Coco suggests, "Could we conduct a fast poll of your employees to see if any of them noticed any strangers in your parking lot on Tuesday?"

"Good idea. Of course we can," replies Charles. He drafts a brief one-question poll. He buzzes Susan at her desk and asks her to come into the conference room. She quickly grasps the thrust of the idea and leaves to prepare a new draft for their review.

It doesn't take Susan long to draw up the draft. She returns to the conference room and the form is finalized.

Charles adds, "Advise anyone who noticed any nonemployees in our parking lot last Tuesday to immediately come up to the conference room and report their observations."

To speed up the distribution of the poll, Susan solicits several other secretaries to help out.

Within fifteen minutes, Andy Sacks, one of the engineering staff, walks into the conference room and announces that the oil change guys were there on Tuesday. Charles shakes his hand and thanks him for his diligence.

Charles says to Coco, "We have a contractual arrangement with King of Oil, an on-site oil change and car wash service. They show up on schedule every month. Let's make them your first stop. I don't suspect them, but their guys may have seen a stranger on our lot last Tuesday."

"Now let's move on to the next subject," Charles continues as he lays the Priority Mail package and the sealed fish bag on the conference table.

"Whoa," blurts out Coco. "That's a sure calling card from the Mafia. I guess we're not finished with the Bianco family."

After looking over the package and noticing the Harborport shipping point, Coco informs Charles that he will pay a visit to the Harborport post office and see what he can turn up.

Charles agrees, and Coco shakes his hand. "I'll keep you posted on this matter as well as the others on my next visit." Coco packs up and departs.

~

The next day, Coco drives up to Harborport and inquires where the post office might be. He is directed to the downtown section of Harborport, right next to the First National Bank on Main Street.

Coco parks his car and takes the Priority Mail package into the post office. He identifies himself to one of the counter staff and asks to speak with the postmaster. John Larson soon emerges from his office, shakes hands with Coco, and introduces himself. He asks how he can be of assistance to him. Coco says he needs some information about their Priority Mail program.

Coco's first question concerns the lack of a complete return address on the package that was sent from this post office to Mr. Charles Caruso. He explains, "You can see that there is neither sender nor a street address on this package. How can your counter staff accept a package so addressed?"

"That's easy," starts the postmaster. "Many post offices now have automated postal centers. The sender merely presses a few buttons and the machine prints out a postage-paid sticker for the sender to affix to the package. The post office staff doesn't get a chance to check for proper identification of the sender."

John Larson goes on, "The sender of this package obviously didn't want to be identified. I wish I could be of more assistance to you and your client. But that's the price we all pay for our electronic technological advancements."

Coco responds, "I appreciate your cooperation and your frankness." He extends his hand to the postmaster. They shake hands and Coco leaves the post office.

Coco is dejected; he thought he was going to uncover some valuable information from the postmaster—to no avail.

~

Coco returns to his office and begins a review of his ever-growing file collection affecting the Caruso family. He lists each event chronologically, along with a synopsis of its current status. The collection starts with the disappearance and killing of the Carusos' cat.

A. The Death of Fluffy. Aside from knowing that the cat was suffocated, little has been uncovered as to the perpetrator of the slaying. Neither the birthday card nor the birthday-gift box yielded any identifiable fingerprints. The case has been referred to the Nassau County District Attorney's office where it is classified as "cold."

B. The Poisoning of Janet Zook. The poison that killed Janet Zook has been identified as the toxic abrin. It is derived from the seed powder of the rosary pea plant. The powder was spread in Mrs. Caruso's home garden. Mrs. Zook weeded the garden a few days before her death as a favor to Mrs. Caruso who was away with her family for a few days. Mrs. Zook inhaled the poison while weeding the garden.

C. Tracing the Deadly Plant. A mail-order flower/plant outlet in northeastern Florida has been found that sells the deadly plant. The company's records confirm a sale of rosary pea plants to a Professor Randolph Anderson. He is the father of the young girl who was killed as a result of the car accident involving Chip Caruso. The connection is still being investigated.

D. Vandalism at the Summerhouse. The Stoney Point police department has been investigating the break-in and vandalism case. To date, they have not accumulated any significant evidence to charge anyone. The case is classified as "open."

E. Mugging of PI Matt Penza. While there is no evidence as to the perpetrators of this crime, everyone knows that they were henchmen for the Bianco Mafia family.

F. The Cut Brake Lines. This investigation is just beginning. What seems irrefutable is that the Giancarlo family is also responsible for this crime. The arrival of the dead fish soon after the lines were cut logically seems to tie the Mafia to this manslaughter case.

G. The Anonymous Fish Package. At least we now have an explanation of how easily a person can send an anonymous Priority Mail package.

~

Before returning to Charles Caruso's office to review the various investigations, Coco contacts the King of Oil Company in Freeport. He makes an appointment to meet with the president of the company.

Coco arrives at the King of Oil offices and meets with Chuck Freeman, their company president. After Coco explains his mission, Chuck Freeman has his office manager bring in the field staff's scheduling charts for the past week. It doesn't take long to zero in on the Caruso Construction stop.

The two men who serviced the Caruso account last Tuesday are identified as Wally Fox and Bobby Quinn. Both are presently out in the field, servicing cars at the headquarters of HouseMaster Franchise Systems in Hempstead. Freeman volunteers, "I'll call them and see if they'll meet you for lunch somewhere. It'll cost you the price of several lunches. Are you game?"

Coco jumps at the thoughtful offer. "That would be great. As you might imagine in a case like this, time is truly of the essence."

Freeman contacts his men and arranges for them to meet with Coco at noon at Carrabba's Restaurant on Hempstead Turnpike just off the Cross Island Parkway. Coco knows exactly where it is and how to get there.

Coco thanks Chuck Freeman for his professionalism and courtesy and heads out to meet the guys.

Just at noon, Coco pulls into the restaurant's parking lot and notices the King of Oil jet-black truck—it would be hard to miss.

He meets the two uniformed men inside the restaurant. After the formalities, they are seated at a quiet corner booth as requested.

Coco calls the waiter over and all three place their orders for lunch. Now the three can talk for a while without interruption.

Coco explains that someone entered the Caruso Construction Company's rear parking lot last Tuesday and sabotaged Charles Caruso's car by cutting its brake lines.

Coco continues, "You fellows were there last Tuesday. That's why we are meeting today."

The young men's faces instantly take on a pale, sullen look.

Coco quickly reassures them. "We know you're not involved in this crime but we want you to think long and hard and see if you can conjure up memories of any strangers in the lot while you were there."

The young men's complexions return to normal.

Bobby Quinn is the first to speak up. "Yes I did see a stranger there last Tuesday."

"At the time I thought it was a bit weird. He wore dark coveralls like ours and a dark baseball cap. He was of average height and weight, as I recall."

Bobby adds, "Oh, one more thing. He was carrying several long-handled instruments with him. That's about it. He was only there for a short time and then he left in a dark-colored sedan. Wait, now that I think about it, those instruments could have been wire cutters."

Coco is delighted. He persists, "Are you sure he was a male? And was there any distinguishing features or characteristics that you recall? Anything at all."

Bobby thinks deeply and responds, "With the coveralls on, I guess I really couldn't tell if the stranger was male or female. I'll tell you one thing though. If the stranger was a girl, she wasn't very well endowed, if you know what I mean."

Coco and Wally smile, and Bobby adds, "I did notice some blond hair jutting out from under his cap."

Coco, who had been taking notes, closes his pad and thanks both young men for their cooperation. He concludes with "Your recollections might just help to locate the brake line cutter and solve this case."

The waiter brings their lunches, and they all enjoy their meals. Coco settles the check and tips the waiter. He also hands each of the men one of his business cards in case anything else comes to mind. Coco shakes their hands and leaves the restaurant.

CHAPTER SIXTEEN

Tuesday dawns with an accompaniment of bright skies and mild temperatures. It's a perfect day for a sightseeing tour of northeastern Pennsylvania.

Irene wakens with unbridled excitement and anticipation of another inspirational day with Jonathan. She wonders how Jonathan and Randolph can share identical genes. They seem so alike from their looks, stature, and facial expressions, to their bright blond hair. Yet from a personality standpoint, they are so diametrically opposed.

Irene's first stop this morning is her friendly Shell gas station. She fills her tank and checks her oil level to prepare for her big trip.

Within an hour, Irene is approaching the town of Milton, home to Sunnyvale Meadows.

At exactly ten o'clock, Irene parks her car and enters the lobby of Sunnyvale Meadows. Knowing Jonathan's suite number, she heads directly to it. She knocks on his door. Jonathan opens the door with a grin on his face and greets Irene, "Good morning, Irene. It's good to see you again. I'm all set to go."

Together they hop into her car and they're off to the races. They follow rural Route 31 north and wind their way through one quaint town after another. When they reach Route 80, they enter it in a westward direction.

Jonathan is still fascinated with heavy traffic. With Route 80's eight lanes of traffic flowing east and west, he comments, "Wow! That's a lot of cars. How do they manage to avoid bumping into each other?"

Irene responds, "It takes a lot of skill and even more luck."

Just south of the town of Stroudsburg, Irene departs Route 80 at exit 313. She quickly merges onto Route 42 north. It's a four-lane highway that's a pleasure to drive in. The fall colors of the leaves are just beginning to appear, further enhancing their experience.

Within half an hour, Irene and Jonathan approach the town of Millville in the uplands of the Pocono Mountains in northeastern Pennsylvania. Keeping their eyes out for signs for Millville Falls, they soon are directed to take a left turn into Millville Falls Road at the next traffic light.

Jonathan is emotionally charged. He can't wait to see what's coming up next. This just might be the most exciting place he has ever visited.

Irene pulls up to the entrance gate of Millville Falls and pays their admission fee. She follows the signs for visitor parking and soon enters a huge parking lot. It looks like it could accommodate several thousand cars.

The entire lot is clearly marked and Irene has no trouble selecting a space close to the park's shuttle tram system. Irene and Jonathan walk over to the tram station and board the next shuttle. Jonathan has never been on a tram before and can hardly contain his excitement.

Almost as soon as the tram leaves the parking lot area, the scenery changes dramatically. They first see a rippling stream of lively white-capped water rushing down from above into Cedar Falls and then into the upper canyon.

"It's incredible," says Jonathan. "I've never seen waterfalls like these before. They're beautiful."

They get off the tram at a "scenic point" and walk along one of the many paths throughout the park. They notice a sign for the park's service area. It mentions the park's restaurant, the Mill Falls Inn.

The Fall Inn is housed in a rustic log-cabin-like lodge. They enter and are escorted to a table near a window overlooking yet another stream. After a hearty lunch, they move into the Inn's hospitality lounge and ease into two stuffed chairs. This is the moment Irene has been waiting for.

Irene begins, "There's something I want to tell you. Randolph and I have separated and will eventually get divorced."

Jonathan looks very surprised. "What happened to cause this?" Jonathan wants to know.

"Well," Irene explains, "Randolph finally admitted that he didn't pick up Erin, our daughter, the night of the accident because he was winning at a faculty poker game and didn't want to leave the game."

Irene continues, "I blew my top when I heard that admission. Erin would be well today if he had kept his promise and picked Erin up that night. I can't ever forgive him for his selfishness that night."

Jonathan jumps in, "I don't blame you one bit. To be honest with you, I always thought that he was hiding something. That's the kind of a creep he is. He should have to pay for his transgression big-time."

"To help get over his betrayal," Irene adds, "I've been seeing my family doctor. He has me on a mood-altering regimen, which seems to be working so I can get on with my life."

"I think I know what you mean. Several months ago, my doctors changed several of my prescriptions. The results have been outstanding in my recovery. It is only because of my doctors and these new medications that I am able to leave Sunnyvale Meadows and enter the outside world, like today. I am beginning to feel like a regular person again."

With broad smiles on their faces, Irene and Jonathan leave the Fall Inn and head back to the tram stop

The wild flowers are blooming everywhere among the varied chiseled boulders. The tram carries them over to another of the highlights of the day—Bridal Veil Falls, a hundred plus feet drop over the Lady Beth Flats.

Again they exit the tram and walk over to a swinging bridge over the Supreme Falls.

Carefully, hand in hand, Jonathan and Irene gingerly step onto the narrow wooden plank bridge designed to accommodate two people side by side. The gentle swaying of the bridge makes Irene question the wisdom in continuing their crossing, but the spectacular view of the Supreme Falls below soon dispels her doubts. To view the thousands and thousands of gallons of silvery water cascading over the edge into the Misty River Cove from that vantage point both exhilarates and terrorizes Irene and Jonathan.

The relief felt in arriving on the other side of the gorge is quickly tempered by the thoughts of the return trip on the bridge. They take a few minutes to savor the breathtaking view before heading back.

Once safely over the gorge, Irene and Jonathan collectively let out sighs of relief and take the tram back to their parking lot. They quickly locate their car and enter it.

Jonathan asks Irene a surprising question. "Do you think I could drive your car for a few minutes in this huge parking lot? There are only a few parked cars in this section of the lot so I don't think I could cause any damage. Please Irene, I'll drive slowly and be very careful," pleads Jonathan.

Since their day has gone so well so far, Irene gives in and agrees to give him a chance.

They switch seats, and Irene speaks, "Put the key in the ignition switch and start the engine. Now shift the car into d, which stands for drive. Now very gently, step on the right acceleration pedal. That forces the car to move forward. The other pedal is your brake."

Jonathan starts the car and moves it forward at a slow speed. He cautiously drives around the lot, avoiding the occasional parked car.

After a test drive of fifteen minutes, Irene instructs Jonathan to return the car to their starting point. He does just that and brings the car to a gentle stop.

"Congratulations, Jonathan," smiles Irene. "I can't believe you've never driven a car before. You drive like a seasoned veteran."

"Thanks, Irene," replies Jonathan. "You're a real friend to me."

The two sightseers head back to Rockland County and Sunnyvale Meadows.

As they drive along, Jonathan remarks, "I'm real sorry that you had to find out what a terrible person my brother really is. I hate him now more than ever."

Irene responds, "At least we have each other to share our contempt of him."

Soon they come up to the flowered entrance to Sunnyvale Meadows. Jonathan thanks Irene again for another great day and gets out of the car.

Irene heads back to her home and reflects on Jonathan's new look. He has been letting his crew cut grow out. With the longer hair, he now really resembles his brother in all ways, except dispositions.

~

The moment she gets home, Irene hears her phone ringing. She rushes into her kitchen and picks up the phone on the fifth ring. "Hello, Irene here," she answers.

"Hi Irene, it's me, Sue. I just wanted to finalize our arrangements for my moving in with you. I have a moving van coming to my apartment tomorrow morning at nine o'clock. It should take them about three hours to pack up everything and get it on the van. That puts us at your house sometime around one o'clock. Does that schedule work for you?"

Irene replies, "Sure. That's fine. I'll see you tomorrow afternoon." Sue concludes the call with, "Okay, that's all set. See you *mañana*."

~

It is indeed the saddest day in the life of Carmella Caruso. She is bidding farewell to one of her most cherished joys—her beautiful flower garden.

Carmella has been amazed by all the red tape involved in having her nursery razed and its contaminated soil removed. Since poisonous elements are involved in this project, the New York State Department of Environmental Protection requires special permits for the removal of the soil and the eventual deposit of it in a regulated landfill. And they mandate that Envira Services, the removal company, also be EPA trained and certified.

It took Carmella almost two months to get to this point. The crew from Envira Services arrives, all decked out in their bright orange hazmat outfits. The special orange plastic containers are all lined up beside the nursery, ready for filling.

Once Carmella signs off on the job, the crew gets started with their shovels and backhoes. Amazingly, they finish up in a little over four hours, load their containers and equipment on their truck, and are on their way.

Carmella's heart is truly broken as she surveys the unbelievable void to the front right of her house. She muses about what's next in store for them in the crazy world of Caruso.

~

Irene's position as a consumer advocate for her company, Sunnyside Foods, has been working out just fine for her and the company. Irene really enjoys the interaction with the consumers of her company's products.

Irene was unsuspecting on her second call on her Friday schedule. Her appointment was set with a Mrs. Roland Sessions of Huntington, Long Island, for eleven o'clock.

Irene arrives on schedule and rings the front doorbell of a 1940s ranch-style house. Mrs. Sessions answers the bell and opens the door. She escorts Irene into a modest living room and offers her a seat. Irene accepts and takes out her recorder and note portfolio. She asks Mrs. Sessions if she has any problem with her recording their conversations. Mrs. Sessions gives her approval, and they are ready to talk.

Mrs. Sessions begins, "Several weeks ago, I cut a coupon out of the newspaper for fifty cents off a package of your My Captain's Table fried clams. I prepared the clams as instructed on the package."

She continues, "We all had a few of the clams including my son Darryl. After taking a bite of the clams, he started to choke uncontrollably. We rushed him to the Emergency Room of Huntington Hospital."

Irene interrupts, "That's awful, Mrs. Sessions. How is Darryl today?"

Mrs. Sessions replies, "The doctors removed a sharp piece of a clamshell from his throat before it could do any serious damage to his esophagus."

Irene jumps in on this bit of good fortune as she was trained. "Mrs. Sessions, we at Sunnyside Foods regret your family's experience with our fried clam product. We would like to offer to cover your family's medical bills once confirmed. We would also like to deliver to you a case of My Captain's Table fried clams so your family can enjoy them often."

Irene concludes with a smile and says, "Does that generous offer please you, Mrs. Sessions?"

Expecting a positive response, Irene is shocked by Mrs. Sessions' snappy comeback.

"No. We want a $100,000 check from your company for causing our family such grief. Sunnyside Foods is a big profitable company that can afford to spend a few dollars to keep an injured customer from going to the press and exposing their shoddy and unsafe products."

Irene counters with "Mrs. Sessions, that sounds a lot like a threat of blackmail. That's a criminal act. Are you sure you want to pursue that course of action?"

As Mrs. Sessions rises to usher Irene out of her house, she adds, "You bet. My lawyer says we have an ironclad case here. So go back to your company and start the ball rolling."

Irene leaves the Sessions' house and, once in her car, writes up the bizarre details of her visit. She will have to see her boss about this shocking turn as soon as possible. She calls his secretary and explains the dilemma. An appointment is set for Monday.

Irene is actually pleased with her handling of this unreasonable consumer. A few months ago, she would have been rattled by someone like Mrs. Sessions and possibly gone to pieces.

CHAPTER SEVENTEEN

It's just past one o'clock when Sue and her moving van and crew arrive at Irene's house. Irene greets them and helps to direct the men to Sue's upstairs bedroom.

Sue is moving into Randolph's old bedroom. Irene had the room thoroughly cleaned and aromatized. It hasn't smelled like a fresh day in spring in many a day. Sue is extremely pleased with how well her furniture and accessories blend with the bedroom and the adjacent bathroom.

Once the moving men and van leave, Irene walks upstairs and into Sue's bedroom with an open bottle of Mumm champagne and two flutes. She pours each of them a glass and proposes a toast.

"Here's to a long and pleasurable time together."

They click glasses, sip the champagne, and hug.

"This could be the start of something big," Irene utters with a coy smile.

~

Now that Sue finally made the big move into Irene's house, she extends her thoughts to her day-to-day existence. Observing Irene's renewed élan and vitality since she started her new job, Sue decides to follow Irene's lead and pursue such a position for herself.

Sue checks the want ads in the Long Island Press newspaper focusing on the sales-help section. One particular offering catches her eye. Metro

Research Inc. is seeking field representatives to sample food products in Long Island supermarkets and record consumer feedback on the products.

Sensing that the position sounded just right for her, Sue calls the listed number and makes an appointment for an interview with John Noone, MRI's regional manager.

Sue meets with Mr. Noone at the Red Hen Diner at the crossroad of Rosyln Road and Old Country Road in East Hempstead. After formalities and ordering some coffee, Mr. Noone details the responsibilities of the position. Before she could begin actual fieldwork, Sue would have to attend a two-day training class at their Flushing offices.

The hours of work are flexible, so Sue opts for the same schedule that Irene has—Monday, Wednesday, and Friday. The pay scale is discussed and agreed upon.

Mr. Noone offers Sue the position and schedules her for the next training class.

They finish their coffee, shake hands, and both leave the diner.

~

Jonathan calls Acme Limo and arranges for another car day with Willie.

~

Robert Thompson, the chemical engineer assigned by the Nassau County District Attorney's office to investigate the unusual circumstances surrounding the death of Janet Zook, has completed his fieldwork and prepared his final summation of his findings and recommendations.

In his final report to the district attorney, Thompson details the results of the autopsy on Mrs. Zook i.e., she was killed by a powerful poison, abrin.

He recounts his trip to northeast Florida to trace the possible source of the poison. He discovers that the rosary pea plant's seeds produce the toxic powder.

Thompson identifies Bountiful Acres in Starke, Florida, as a seller of this species of plant and the shipper of several of these plants to one Randolph Anderson, director of Chemical Engineering at Strafford College in North Woodlane.

Thompson states that he has gone as far with this investigation as his experience and background can take him.

He feels that he has definitely identified this case as one of homicide or at least manslaughter. He states that the time is right to transfer this investigation to the homicide detective bureau.

The district attorney reviews the entire file and case with Robert Thompson and the chief of the homicide detective bureau. They all agree with Thompson's logic and recommendation. The DA thanks Thompson for his fine work and passes the investigation file on to the homicide detective bureau for reassignment and follow-up.

~

One balmy evening, Irene suggests that Sue join her for a soothing splash in the heated pool. Sue quickly agrees and both women head up stairs to their bedrooms to change into their bathing suits.

Once changed, Sue heads outside to the swimming pool while Irene goes to the outdoor lighting panel in her den and flips on the pool lights and the backyard lighting.

When the lights burst into brightness, Sue is shocked to see a poolside radio lying at the bottom of the pool in the shallow end with a connected extension cord coiling up and out of the pool.

Sue screams to Irene, "Don't go near the pool! You'll be electrocuted. Look down there, there's a radio lying at the bottom of the pool, and it's live."

Irene responds, "Oh my gosh. Thank God you noticed that before we jumped into the pool. It would have been curtains for both of us. Don't move, I'm going to see where that extension cord is plugged in and unplug it. It'll only take me a few minutes to locate it and deactivate it."

Irene quickly accomplishes her goal and returns to Sue standing by the pool. "We're safe now," offers Irene as she puts a bit of her right foot into the pool to reassure Sue. She smiles with a sigh of relief, "Whew."

Hand in hand, the women jump into the deep end of the pool. The comfortable water temperature soon soothes their jagged psyches. They swim around for a while and then loll on several inflated floats in the pool.

As they are drifting along, Sue raises the obvious question of who could have set this potential death trap.

Irene responds, "God only knows. Of course, you know me. I always suspect Randolph."

They eventually climb out of the pool, towel off, and enter the house. Irene shuts off the outdoor lighting.

The hour is now late and they each head for their bedroom, shower, and retire.

Unbeknownst to Sue, when Irene went over to locate and unplug the "live" extension cord, it wasn't plugged in at all.

~

Randolph thoroughly reviews the divorce materials that Irene had given him the day he moved out of their house. He has little disagreement with most of her suggestions and desires. He won't complain about any of it at the present time, primarily because he knows that their divorce proceedings are at least a year or so off. He'll have lots of time to fine-tune her calculations. Randolph signs the required forms and sends the original to Irene.

Recently he has been feeling quite frustrated with the realization that those terrible Carusos and especially that rotten kid of theirs have gotten away with the murder of his daughter and caused him immeasurable personal guilt and misery.

Randolph wants his pound of flesh. The only thing that seems to matter to the Carusos is money. So maybe that's another way of avenging Erin's death. We'll sue them for criminal negligence and take them to the bank.

As an afterthought, Randolph realizes that they will have to move on the lawsuit while they are still a legally married couple.

Randolph calls Irene and fills her in on his thinking, especially about the lawsuit against the Carusos. He goes on, "I'm thinking of demanding a million dollars. What do you think?"

Irene excitedly responds, "Why not? They cost us our little baby. And she was priceless."

Randolph concludes the call with an offer to check out prospective trial attorneys.

~

Coco calls Charles at his office and sets an appointment time to update him on the latest on all the investigative work.

The next day, Coco arrives at Charles's office on schedule and is directed to his conference room. Charles is there already and they get right into it.

Coco starts with "I've prepared a summary of the cases we've been working on. I'll quickly recap each and bring you up to speed on each of them." Coco slides his report across the conference table to Charles.

"As you can see, we've gotten nowhere on discovering much about your daughter's cat. You can assume, I believe, that the whole episode was orchestrated by a real sadist with a major disconnect with your family.

"Next, the death of your neighbor, Janet Zook, has been officially classified as a homicide or manslaughter by the Nassau County DA.

"We know, as a result of her autopsy, that she died as a result of her inhalation of the poison abrin. That potent poison is derived from the rosary pea plant. The powder from the plant's seeds was spread on the soil of your wife's flower garden.

"We have traced a possible supplier of these toxic plants to an outlet in Florida. And their records confirm that a shipment of six of these deadly plants was processed and sent to one Randolph Anderson. He is the director of Chemical Engineering at Strafford College in North Woodlane. And he is the father of the girl killed as a result of that auto accident in which Chip was involved.

"This could be the big break we have been hoping for. I am following this clue line as is the Nassau County Homicide Bureau.

"The next issue is a real poser. The Stony Point Police Department is still actively investigating the vandalism of your home. At this point, they don't even have any substantive evidence or any persons of interest.

"Moving on to the mugging of one of my operatives, I don't think this will ever be solved. But we all know who called the shots on it.

"The most recent threat to your life, the cutting of your brake lines, is still hot. We have made some headway on identifying the perpetrator. I contacted the King of Oil Company and interviewed their two service men who were in your lot that day with what looked like wire cutters.

"They couldn't precisely identify what appeared to be a white male in black coveralls. But they did note that the stranger had blond hair under his baseball cap.

"Now we have to ferret this guy out. I'm convinced that someone involved in this circle of events over the past number of months knows of him. Everyone involved has to be quizzed about the guy with the blond hair.

"And finally, my visit with your Harborport postmaster didn't shed any light on the sender of that dead fish package to your office, not that there's much doubt about the sender's identity."

When Coco concludes his presentation, Charles thanks him and they shake hands.

"Keep me posted, Coco. I'll do some checking with my family on that blond guy," concludes Charles.

"Okay," responds Coco. "I'll be checking in with you." Coco packs up and leaves the conference room.

~

Jonathan shows up as planned at the Acme Limo office and is welcomed by Willie.

"What's our plans for today, Jonathan?" asks Willie. "It's a surprise," responds Jonathan as he hops into the front passenger seat of their regular wheels.

As they drive out of the town of Milton, Jonathan opens up a bit and divulges a part of his plan. "First off, I would like to drive over to Giants Stadium in the Meadowlands." Willie has been there many times and knows exactly how to get there.

There are no football games or any other activities going on at the stadium that afternoon. It looks like an abandoned facility. The huge parking lots engulfing the stadium look like a distant moonscape in their starkness.

Willie speaks, "Okay Jonathan, here we are. What's the master plan?" Jonathan asks Willie to park the car so they can discuss something important to Jonathan. Willie promptly complies and shuts off the car's motor.

Jonathan begins, "I trust you, Willie. I feel that I can confide in you as a true friend. That's why we are here today. Now that I have recovered my mental and physical health to a large measure, I want to make up for all those lost years. I would like to start by learning to drive a car. Then I want to obtain my social security card and finally a driver's license. I'll give you a thousand dollars out of my trust fund if you will help me accomplish these goals. What do you think, Willie?"

Willie sits motionless for a few minutes mulling over Jonathan's generous offer. He replies, "Sure, Jonathan. You deserve your freedom. I think of you as a friend and would be glad to help you out. I can practice parking and driving with you until you are ready for your driver's license test. That's not so difficult.

And I'll do some online checking back at the office on obtaining a Social Security card."

"You're the best, Willie," beams Jonathan.

They spend the next few hours practicing in the Meadowlands parking lots and then return home.

CHAPTER EIGHTEEN

Surprisingly, it took two of the Metro NY television stations several days to pick up on the bizarre suburban poisoning of a Long Island housewife and also the weird auto collision caused because a classic car's brakes lines had been cut deliberately. Now the stations are making up for lost time by emphasizing the common thread that connects these diverse stories, the involvement of a prominent Long Island family—the Carusos of Harborport.

Both stations are playing footage of the scene of Charles Caruso's auto collision on an exit ramp of the Southern State Parkway. Each time the story is aired, it is immediately followed by images of the Carusos' splendid house and the vacant lot adjacent to the house where the deadly garden once blossomed.

At the conclusion of each newscast, viewers are encouraged to contact the Nassau County Detective Bureau at (555) 400-CLUE (2583) if they have any pertinent information about either case.

~

Jonathan is so excited about the big turn of events in his life that he has to share the good news with one of his new friends, Irene.

He locates the card Irene gave him months ago with her address and telephone number on it and places a call to her.

"Hi, Irene," Jonathan gleefully announces. "It's me, Jonathan. I have some exciting news to share with you. Remember last week when we went up to the waterfalls and you let me drive your car around that huge parking lot? Well, I met with my car friend, Willie, yesterday, and he has agreed to teach me how to drive, so I can pass the driver's license test. And he is also going help me obtain a social security card as well. Isn't that wonderful?"

Irene responds, "You bet, Jonathan. That's fantastic news. You'll now have opportunities to get out and really explore the outside world."

She continues, "You know I don't think you'll need to apply for a new Social Security card. I believe your parents applied for them when you and Randy were born. Let me check this out with Randy. I'll get back to you in a day or so."

"Thanks, Irene. You're a real good person. I'll talk to you again soon," responds Jonathan as he hangs up.

~

Randolph calls Irene to inform her that he thinks he has found the perfect trial attorney to handle their lawsuit against the Carusos. "His name is Raymond J. Cotter, and he is an associate professor of law at Strafford College. He has been practicing law for over twenty years and knows his way around the local court system. He has a most successful litigation record. I took the liberty of setting up a meeting with him at his office in Mineola next Wednesday evening at eight o'clock. Are you amenable to that?"

Irene replies, "Sounds good to me, give me his address and phone number in case I get lost." Randolph complies.

"Okay," says Irene. "That's all set. Oh, by the way, didn't you once tell me that your parents obtained Social Security cards for you and your brother when you were born?"

Randolph confirms that they did get their Social Security cards at birth but wants to know why she is asking.

"Sue and I were discussing social security coverage the other day and she said that you couldn't get a Social Security card at birth," responds Irene.

"Oh, okay," responds Randolph.

"Be talking to you," mutters Irene as she hangs up the phone.

~

Now that Sue has completed her training course for her new position, she's ready for actual fieldwork. For the first week, she meets veteran representatives at various supermarkets and observes their sampling techniques. Assuming everything goes well, Sue will then go solo the following week.

On Friday of each week, the office faxes each representative their personal schedule for the upcoming week. Each Monday morning, the representatives' basic materials are delivered to their assigned supermarket. They receive their folding card table, table cover, samples, and promotional pieces as well as their bib aprons. The representatives are responsible for their own appearance and attire.

At the completion of their workweek, each representative must fax into headquarters a detailed report form outlining their sampling volume and feedback.

Sue is eagerly anticipating her new experience. It should help her ward off those negative thoughts that still plague her, especially those of Randolph. She is looking forward to thinking more positively. Dr. Schmidt, her psychologist, will be pleased with her for being so proactive.

~

Within three weeks, Jonathan receives his replacement Social Security card and applies for a learner's driver's license. He'll be ready for his driver's license test in another week. He calls Irene and Willie to tell them the good news and to again thank them for being there for him.

~

The Stony Pines Police Department's investigation into the vandalism at the Carusos' house has been concluded. The investigation uncovered the following evidentiary matters:

- The Eye See You house watch company reported that the house alarm system was activated earlier that Saturday after their morning visit. Since the system is monitored around the clock, the security company would have been alerted. There was no alarm on Saturday.
- Charles Caruso Jr.'s car was witnessed at the house on Halloween eve by the Eye See You technician as he drove by.
- A blood smear on a shard from the kitchen door's glass matched the DNA of Charles Caruso Jr.

- There was a light black smudge on Charles Caruso Jr.'s right index finger. It could have occurred while spray painting the message on the TV screen.

As he is driving between sales calls, Chip's cell phone rings. He is surprised to hear the voice of Detective Kuhn from the Stony Pines Police Department. The detective informs Chip that they are making progress regarding the break-in and vandalism of his family's summerhouse case. The detective wants to review their findings with him.

Although taken aback a smidgeon by the surprise call, Chip readily agrees. They set an appointment for an afternoon later in the week.

~

Chip pulls up to the Stony Pines Police Station, parks his car, and walks into the building. He marches up to the desk sergeant, identifies himself, and asks to see Detective Ryan Kuhn, who is expecting him.

Detective Kuhn comes out to the lobby and leads Chip down a hall and into an interrogation room. To Chip's surprise, Kuhn reads him his Miranda rights and then begins, "We have reason to believe that the break-in and vandalism at your family's summer home were not perpetrated by an outsider. Our investigation has uncovered significant evidence which points to you as the orchestrator of the entire affair. And we know we can prove it in a court of law."

Kuhn continues, "Before you say anything, let me explain how these things play out. If you cooperate with us and admit your involvement, we will recommend leniency to the court. On the other hand, if you want to play hardball, we are prepared to play the same game. You could be facing several multiple felony charges including vandalism, breaking and entry, and the most serious of all, falsification of an official police report. Conviction on any one of these felony charges could mandate prison time."

Detective Kuhn goes on, "On the other hand, if you fully cooperate with us and admit your involvement, we could see these felony charges reduced to misdemeanors."

He finishes his pitch with a question for Chip, "So what's your poison? Cooperate or contest?"

Chip who has been listening intensely to Detective Kuhn, asks a question, "If I cooperate, can this be just between us. Can I keep my family out of it?"

Kuhn answers, "I can't guarantee that. The owners of vandalized properties are always officially notified of the outcome of these cases. Which way do you want to go?"

"I'll confess," Chip readily agrees. "The whole thing started as a Halloween prank and got out of control. I'm sorry. I'd really appreciate anything you can do for me." Kuhn adds, "You'll be notified of your court date and time. It will be heard in night court."

They shake hands and Chip leaves with Detective Kuhn's words ringing in his ears, "You're doing the right thing. In the meantime, don't leave the state."

~

Charles Caruso waits until his family has finished dinner, to raise the issue of the blond-haired stranger who was seen at the Caruso Construction parking lot. He tells his family that the detectives who are looking into the cutting of the brake lines of his Chevy suspect that the culprit might have bright blond hair.

He asks each family member to think real hard to see if anyone can recall a boy or man that they may have encountered who had blond hair.

Neither Carmella nor C. C. can recall such a person with blond hair.

Charles looks over at Chip who offers, "Remember back when you asked about the guy with the blond hair? I brought up the name of Professor Anderson who has blond hair and said that I had encountered him at his daughter's funeral. He accosted me there and threatened to kill me."

Charles chimes in, "I do remember you saying that. I'll have Coco check him out and find out where he lives and works."

"Thanks, everyone," Charles concludes. "Let's have dessert."

~

On Wednesday evening, Irene is the first to arrive at Attorney Cotter's office. She parks her car and waits for Randolph to show up. Ten minutes later, Randolph arrives, and they walk over to Cotter's office. With minimum conversation, they agree to subjugate their intense dislike and distrust for each other so as not to affect the outcome of their upcoming litigation.

As the Andersons enter Cotter's office, he ambles out of his private office to greet them, "C'mon in to my office and we can get started."

He introduces himself to Irene; Randolph already recognizes him from school.

"I understand that you wish to pursue a legal action against the family whose son and automobile were involved in an accident that eventually cost your daughter her life. I'm sorry to hear that. Am I correct about the lawsuit?"

Irene is a bit surprised at the appearance and demeanor of Raymond Cotter. She was expecting a hard-nosed lawyer in the mold of James Wood when he starred on the television show *Shark*. Instead she sees a kindly older gentleman more like Andy Griffith's *Matlack*. She wonders if he will be sharp enough to do battle with an army of hotshot lawyers that the Carusos are sure to throw at them. She'll have to talk with Randolph about her concerns.

Randolph responds to Cotter's question, "You're right. The Carusos' son was driving the car that crashed into Irene's car."

Cotter is recording pertinent comments on a legal pad as they move on. He opens with "We'll have to do a lot of questioning and probing to determine the validity and strength of your suit. Let me start with the accident itself. Whose fault was it?"

Irene and Randolph look at each other to see who will answer. Irene leads, "Go ahead, Randolph, you answer."

Randolph replies, "The boy's car plowed into Irene's car, and he was drinking before the accident."

Cotter asks, "Was he charged with a DUI?" Randolph responds, "At first, he was charged with a DUI, but his lawyers got it reduced to a charge of reckless driving."

"Okay, how old was he at that time?"

"We really don't know precisely. We do know he had just graduated from college, so that would put him in the twenty-one-to-twenty-two-year-old bracket."

Cotter raises his hand and says that there are a lot of unknowns in the case that make it near impossible to build a solid case at the time. He offers, "I recommend that you authorize me to employ a private investigator to delve into all these key elements of your case and provide us with solid information."

Both Irene and Randolph nod in unison. They can understand the logic behind that recommendation.

Randolph asks, "How much will the private investigator cost?"

Cotter replies, "My regular PI charges forty dollars per hour, portal-to-portal, plus any expenses incurred. He is a real professional and won't waste any time. You can count on that."

Raymond is first to agree, "Sounds all right to me. What do you think, Irene?" She nods her agreement.

Cotter wraps up their initial session with "It'll take a week or so for our PI to develop a preliminary outline of our evidence. I'll see Randolph at school and tell him when we get together again."

Irene and Randolph shake Cotter's hand and leave his office.

CHAPTER NINETEEN

"Finger of birth-strangled babe ditch deliver'd by the drab, make the gruel thick and slab; add thereto a tiger's cauldron for ingredients of our cauldron."

"Double, double toil and trouble; fire burn and cauldron bubble."

"Bubble Macbeth indeed. Let the Caruso cauldron boil and overflow; and scorch the evildoers, high and low."

~

Jonathan has been practice driving with Willie almost every day. Willie thinks that Jonathan is ready to take and pass his driver's license exam and road test; Jonathan agrees with him and schedules a date for the written exam and the road test.

~

Coco drives up to the campus of Strafford College. At the main reception area, he approaches one of the receptionists, identifies himself, and inquires about one of their staff, Professor Randolph Anderson. Coco assures the receptionist that this is just a routine call and it's nothing to get alarmed about. He is advised that Professor Anderson is the school's director of Chemical Engineering and can be located at the Sarah Slevin Center for Advanced Studies on the far end of the campus. Coco receives driving directions and heads over to the center.

Armed with a black-and-white photograph of Professor Anderson clipped from a newspaper, Coco feels confident he will be able to identify the professor if he comes across him. Equipped with his Canon EOS 20D camera with telephoto lens, Coco parks his car and walks across to the center.

The 11:50 AM class-ending buzzer goes off. The doorways are instantly jammed with fleeing students rushing to the cafeteria across the quad.

Coco patiently waits for the emergence of Professor Anderson.

Sure enough, after the vast majority of hungry students have vacated the center, a very proper-looking academic with bright blond hair comes ambling down the hallway toward Coco. The professor seems to be in a discussion with another professor.

Coco steps back into an alcove and snaps multiple pictures of the professor. Coco decides to follow him for a while to see if he approaches his car. Professor Anderson does leave the center through the automatic double exit doors leading out to the parking lot.

Once the professor gets to his car, Coco snaps additional pictures of his car (a late model Cadillac Escalade) and its license plate. Coco decides to trail the professor's car. Maybe he is finished for the day and heading home. Within about fifteen minutes, the professor pulls into a driveway on a quiet street. Coco takes a few pictures of the house and notes the address.

Content with his efforts in locating and identifying Professor Anderson, his car, and his residence, Coco drives down the professor's tree-lined street heading back to his own office.

~

As agreed, Willie arrives at Sunnyvale Meadows at ten o'clock in the morning. He will drive Jonathan to the Division of Motor Vehicles office in Munsey for his driver's license exam and test drive.

Willie drives Jonathan to the DMV office, parks his car, and gives Jonathan the car keys. Jonathan enters the building and joins the line for license exams.

In less than an hour, Jonathan has completed and passed his written exam. Currently, he is number four on the line for the road test.

At last, his name is called, and he meets his test driver. Together they go outside, get into Willie's car, and start the test drive. It only takes thirty minutes to complete. When they return to the DMV office, his test driver congratulates him on his successful test drive.

Jonathan has passed both portions of the process. He is informed that his license will be mailed to him within the next week.

Willie shakes Jonathan's hand and hugs him. The newly licensed Jonathan drives Willie back to Sunnyvale Meadows, very carefully.

~

The next morning, Chip stops at his local bank and withdraws two thousand dollars from his graduation gifts account. He leaves the bank with a certified check in that amount. Armed with the check, Chip heads out to Stony Point and the court office to finalize his guilty plea settlement.

Chip leaves with a copy of his court papers securely in hand, feeling an overwhelming sense of relief. In his heart, he knows that this was more than a prank; it was an act of retaliation against his father.

~

Mary Johnston, director of Nassau County Homicide Division, appoints James Sullivan, a veteran homicide detective in the department, to follow up on Detective Robert Thompson's preliminary investigation and report on the suspicious death of Janet Zook.

Detective Sullivan gets right into the case. He spends hours reading and digesting Detective Thompson's thorough report with attachments. His first forward step is to make a list of the leading characters in this case with his own notations of seemingly pertinent actions, motives, or suspicions of them.

His initial list of persons of interest includes the following:

- Janet Zook. The deceased. Why was she asked to *actually* weed Carmella Caruso's garden? Carmella was only going to be away for a few days. The weeding could have waited until Carmella returned.
- John Zook. The deceased's husband. What was their relationship like? Does he have a chemical background or knowledge of poisons?
- Carmella Caruso. The owner of the toxic garden. Did she have a reason to scare or kill her neighbor, Janet? Why did she require her neighbor to pull weeds and expose herself to the poison powder? Why didn't she also exhibit effects of the poison?

- Charles Caruso. Carmella's husband. How's their relationship? Did he have anything to do with the garden?
- Chip Caruso. Son. Living at home? How's his relationship with his parents. What does he do for a living? Does he have a drinking problem? Has anyone obtained a copy of the accident report and the negotiations with the county to reduce the charges against him from DUI to reckless driving?
- Cara. Daughter. Did anyone hate her first cat, Fluffy? Did any of the Carusos' neighbors or children notice anyone petting or paying attention to her cat?
- Professor Anderson. Accident victim's father. He seems like the most suspicious of all. With his blond hair, he's been popping up all over the place—at the Caruso Company's parking lot, at the Carusos' gated community. And he has the best motive of all—retaliation for his daughter's death.
- Irene Anderson. Accident victim's mother. How's their marital relationship going? She certainly has as strong a motive as her husband. Where do they live? Is she emotionally stable?
- Coco Crandel. Charles Caruso's private investigator. He must know a lot at this point. How open will he be to answering a few questions? Sounds like one of my first calls.

Sullivan's first phone call is to an old buddy of his in the Nassau County DA office, Bill Wilson. "Hi, Bill, it's Jim Sullivan. I need a favor from you. I'm working a case that revolves around a fatal auto accident back in May. One of the two cars involved was driven by Charles Caruso's son, Chip."

He adds, "Initially the Caruso boy was charged with a DUI. His lawyers were able to plead his DUI down to a charge of reckless driving. And that's where I need your assistance."

Sullivan goes on, "I need a copy of the official accident report as well as a copy of the plea arguments and resolution. I could go through official channels and request the same information but that could take weeks. I need this information sooner than that. Do you think you can help me out on this?"

Wilson responds, "Sure, Sully. I don't see a problem expediting your request. Let me check into it. I'll call you if I have any problem with it."

"Thanks, Bill. I really appreciate this," concludes Jim.

~

Within a few days, a certified mail package arrives at Sullivan's desk. He opens it and reviews its contents. It's exactly what he requested of his buddy, Bill Wilson.

The accident report doesn't shed much light on the culpability factor of either party. Both cars and drivers seem to be at fault in one way or another.

Of course, the fact that Chip Caruso had been drinking for a while before the accident tips the scales of blame toward him. However, as Sullivan reads on, he sees that Mrs. Irene Anderson, the other driver, was distracted at the time of impact by a cell phone call from her best friend. That certainly helps balance the scale. And she did run a red light at the accident intersection.

Having read these reports thoroughly, Sullivan decides that he must interrogate Mrs. Anderson and her best friend, Sue Greene. He is able to track down Mrs. Anderson and obtain her home telephone number. Assuming she works all day, he waits until evening to call her.

"Hello, Mrs. Anderson. I'm William Sullivan of the Nassau County Investigative Services (that sounds better than mentioning homicide). I'm following up on your accident back in May. We would like to close out the case, and you can help." Sullivan asks, "Could we meet for lunch someday soon and talk? I'll treat."

Irene is a bit rattled by the request but is afraid to give him the impression that she is concealing something. She replies, "Of course. Pick a diner or restaurant in the Hempstead area, and I'll meet you on Thursday."

They agree on a well-known diner and set the time for twelve noon.

~

Jonathan almost can't believe his good fortune when he sees an envelope in his mail from the New York Division of Motor Vehicles. He quickly tears open the envelope and marvels at the sight of his NY State driver's license. After fawning over his accomplishment, he puts the treasured new license in his wallet for safekeeping.

He calls Willie and tells him the good news. Jonathan's next step is to secure a long-term rental on a decent car. He asks Willie if he can help him with this.

Willie cheerfully announces that his father's company, Acme Limo, is also in the car rental business. Willie can offer Jonathan a good, reliable car at a reasonable rate. Willie suggests that Jonathan grab the noon shuttle to downtown and meet him at the Acme offices.

Jonathan agrees and meets Willie at the Acme offices that afternoon. Willie already has several cars lined up for Jonathan to check out. He immediately takes to a four-year-old blue Saturn Vue. After taking it for a test drive, Jonathan signs the rental and insurance papers. Proudly, Willie hands Jonathan the car keys and registration papers.

Jonathan again thanks Willie for all his help and drives off.

~

It's Thursday evening, and the Stony Pines night court is in session, the honorable John R. Reynolds presiding. Chip is scheduled to appear before the judge in slot number 9. At a little after nine o'clock, the court clerk announces the case against Charles A. Caruso Jr.

Chip comes before the judge, and the charges are read by the clerk. The judge asks him how he pleads. Chip responds, "Guilty, your honor." The judge asks if he understands the implications of such a plea. Chip replies in the affirmative.

The judge accepts his plea and assesses Chip a fine of two thousand dollars and pounds his gavel to indicate case closed. Chip walks over to the court clerk and signs the official court record. The clerk advises him that the entire fine must be paid within three days.

CHAPTER TWENTY

It's Monday morning and the start of Sue's first day of fieldwork. Sue awakens with a sense of excitement tinged with a dash of apprehension. After breakfast with Irene and her pooch, Alfie, she heads out to her first supermarket assignment at a Foodarama Supermarket in Merrick.

Upon arriving at the Foodarama Supermarket, Sue introduces herself to the store manager and then locates her display materials and product samples. Her station today is in the dairy aisle near the refrigerated cheese department. This week she will be sampling and couponing a party dip product, Fiesta Cheese and Herb Delights.

Her maiden day goes by without incident. Many passing shoppers stop at her stand and sample her wares. They seem pleased, and she notices quite a few of them going over to the cheese section and selecting a package of her product. She feels good.

~

Professor Randolph Anderson's new semester is off to a good start. He is teaching Organic Chemistry 106 and Chemical Reaction Analysis 110. With a student enrollment of over 190, each course will be presented in two sessions.

Interestingly, his new student pal, Greg Thurber, is enrolled in one of his Organic Chemistry 106 classes. Randolph is pleased to maintain their blossoming relationship.

~

Irene decides to attend another MADD meeting on her own. She has missed the last three meetings. All the attendees are pleased to see her again; they're all curious about how things are going for her. After the meeting gets started, the moderator asks Irene to fill everyone in on how life is treating her.

With pleasure, Irene addresses the group, starting off with the news of her pending divorce plans. She explains what caused the big blowup and his moving out. The audience almost seems pleased with that news.

Irene goes on to describe the two attempts on her life and how her friend, Sue Greene, who now lives with her, saved her life each time. Irene describes the attempts. First there was the garage door blockage with the cement blocks and then there was the swimming pool electricity threat. Some of the audience question whether her husband could have been behind the failed attempts. Their rationale centers on their belief that he couldn't be responsible since he would be the most obvious suspect. One of the ladies raises the possibility that her lifesaver, Sue Greene, could be a viable suspect; she was there at each attempt. Irene's jaw drops at such a suggestion. Sue is her long-term friend and confidant, but she does have her own issues.

The moderator asks about her husband's twin brother, Jonathan. Irene replies, "Yes, Jonathan and I have developed a bit of a bond over the past few months. He is the antithesis of his brother."

In conclusion, Irene mentions that she and her quasi husband are in the process of filing a lawsuit against the tipsy driver of the other car and his family in her tragic collision.

The group is pleased to hear this news. They all wish Irene good luck and offer their services if she needs any support.

~

Irene and Randolph meet at Attorney Raymond Cotter's office to participate in a strategy session with him and his chosen Private Investigator, Jack Martini.

After introductions, Cotter rolls out a large chalkboard and announces, "Jack has been reviewing what information we have so far. He was able to obtain a copy of the police department's case file on the fatal car crash as well as the district attorney's files relating to the negotiations that lead to their dropping of the DUI charges against Chip Caruso for a lesser charge of reckless driving. Based on what we now know, I would like to develop a preliminary potential plaintiff's witness list and write their names on this board. These will be the people who might be the most helpful in making our case."

He continues, "So let's get started. How about the policeman who was among the first on the scene of the accident? I think his name is Baggins. He was the officer who actually charged Chip Caruso with a DUI. What do you all think?"

Randolph responds, "He sounds like a big plus for our side. What was his basis for the DUI charge?"

Jack Martini answers, "When Officer Baggins administered the Caruso kid the BAT—that's the Breath Analysis Test—he registered a 1.6—twice the threshold of being judged intoxicated. His lawyers argued that the BAT equipment hadn't been recalibrated recently and was inaccurate, thereby negating the entire test and its results."

Randolph adds, "We should be talking with Officer Baggins. He can tell us more about young Caruso's physical condition and mental state at the time of the accident."

"Okay, he's on the list," states Cotter. "I'd like to now address the selection of several other possible witnesses. In cases like this where young people are involved, I have found that maternal grandmothers can be very cooperative and reveal valuable family information if handled gently with respect. The wife's mother is usually more connected with her grandchildren than is the mother of the husband. Often almost acting as a surrogate mother, the maternal grandmother has a better insight into the family dynamics and is more likely to take stands and express her opinion especially when it comes to any of the grandchildren."

Cotter concludes with "We won't bother attempting to interview any of the grandfathers. They usually are more guarded and secretive in a case like this."

PI Martini adds, "In the police report, it was noted that, before the accident, Chip Caruso had been drinking with some school buddies at the Last Call, a local sports bar. I'd like to pay that bar a call and see if I can shake loose a few witnesses who can attest to Caruso's lack of sobriety when he left the bar that evening."

Everyone nods their approval. Cotter closes with "This will get us off and running. We'll keep you posted on our progress. Have a good evening."

As Randolph and Irene walk back to their cars, Irene reluctantly acknowledges that their attorney is far sharper than she first thought. Randolph is pleased with her admission.

~

On Thursday at noon, Irene meets Detective James Sullivan of the Nassau County Homicide Division outside the Bluebay Diner. He asks for and receives a quiet rear booth. After ordering lunch, Detective Sullivan begins, "I've been assigned the task of investigating the apparent homicide of Janet Zook. I'm sure you've heard about the case. Mrs. Zook was a neighbor of Mrs. Charles Caruso in Harborport, Long Island. You should recognize the Caruso name. Her son, Charles Jr., was the other party involved in that awful car accident back last May. Am I making sense to you?"

"Yes," Irene replies. "I know about the Carusos and I've heard about the poisoning of that lady. How can I help you with your investigation?"

Sullivan answers, "I'm not entirely sure at this point. But since I will be asking you questions about a potential homicide, I do have to read you your Miranda rights."

"What?" blurts Irene. "Am I a suspect? What's going on here?"

Sullivan attempts to calm her, "No. no. You're not a suspect. The Miranda rights are read for your protection. It basically assures you the right to legal representation at any time. You'll understand better when you hear them. Can I proceed?"

Hesitatingly Irene agrees and he reads her rights.

Sullivan begins his interrogation, "Your husband's name is Randolph and he is the director of Chemical Engineering at Strafford College, right?" Irene nods.

"As the director of Chemical Engineering, he knows about poison plants and teaches courses dealing with toxic plants, does he not?" Irene responds in the affirmative.

"Did a package of poisonous plants arrive at your home sometime in May of this year from a grower in Florida?" Irene responds, "He did receive a package of plants from Florida back sometime in May. He took the package to his workshop, and I saw him working on some of the plants with gloves and a face mask. I really don't know what he was doing."

"Okay," continues Sullivan. "Let me touch on another subject. Are you and Professor Anderson still living under the same roof?"

Irene hesitates in answering; she wonders if that's any of his damn business. She quickly relents and replies, "We are actually separated at this time and probably will divorce next year."

Sullivan adds, "I'm sorry to hear that. When did he move out of your home?"

"Just two weeks ago," answers Irene.

"Thanks for meeting with me and being so responsive. Now let's enjoy our lunches."

They finish their meals and depart.

~

A few days later, Detective Sullivan calls Irene at home. When she answers, he offers, "Hello, this is Detective Sullivan. I appreciated our time together the other day. Now I'm trying to contact Sue Greene. I thought you might be able to help me."

"Sure," answers Irene. "Actually, Sue, who is a dear friend of mine, moved in with me when my husband moved out. She's not home right now. I'll give you her cell phone number." Irene does and he thanks her.

The next day, Sullivan calls Sue. He explains his mission and asks her to meet him for a cup of coffee. They set an appointment for 3:00 PM next Tuesday at the Coffee Spot in the South Island Mall.

At their appointed time and place, Detective Sullivan and Sue Greene meet. They sit at a convenient bench and begin their dialogue. Sullivan starts with his reading of her Miranda rights to her. Unlike Irene, she accepts the reading and they move on. He asks, "How long have you and Irene been friends?" Sue responds, "I guess about twenty years or so."

Sullivan continues, "When you called her on her cell phone the night of the accident, what was the upsetting news that jarred her so?"

Sue confesses, "I told her that my husband and her friend had just been diagnosed with a case of advanced Multiple sclerosis. She was so upset she dropped her cell phone and gasped out loud."

Sullivan moves on to another subject, "You know her husband, Randolph, don't you?"

"As long as they've been married," Sue answers.

"What caused their breakup?"

Sue frowns as she responds, "Irene blamed Randolph for the death of their only child, Erin. He had promised to pick her up after her dance lesson that evening in his rugged Cadillac Escalade. Irene felt that Erin would still be alive if his big car had picked her up instead of her little car. He got involved in a faculty poker game that evening and refused to leave it to pick up his daughter. They ended up blaming each other for Erin's death and would end up hating each other. I actually think he has been trying to kill Irene ever since."

"How so?" Sullivan queries.

"Well, in the last few months, Irene has barely escaped two threats on her life. Once she was trapped in her garage with her car's engine running, spewing deadly carbon monoxide gas. Someone had propped several concrete blocks up against the garage doors, preventing their opening. Then a few weeks ago, a live electrical line was dropped into her backyard pool."

Sullivan asks, "Why do you think it was her husband?"

"Who else?" replies Sue.

Sullivan asks another question, "Can you think of any other link between her husband and any of the Carusos?" Sue ponders the question for a few seconds and takes a sip of her coffee before responding, "I remember attending the funeral services for their daughter Erin. At the close of the services, Randolph recognized Chip Caruso in the gathering. He rushed him and pushed him to the ground while announcing for all to hear that he will kill him."

Sullivan makes a special notation after that disclosure and adds, "Anything else you think might impact this investigation?"

Sue breathes deeply and answers, "I don't know if this is important but did you know that Irene's husband, Randolph, has an identical twin brother? His name is Jonathan. Both Irene and I have spent a fair amount of time with him over the last few months."

Sue goes on, "Jonathan hates his twin. He blames him for a childhood swing accident which caused him certain brain damage and long-term confinement at Sunnyvale Meadows in Rockland County. His disdain for his brother has intensified since the automobile accident. He also blames his brother for killing poor little Erin by not picking her up that fateful night. I'm afraid that Irene is partially responsible for Jonathan's dire attitude. She told him of Randolph's negligence that night. Jonathan also blames the Caruso kid for drinking and driving, as well as his negligent parents for not supervising him closer."

Sullivan finishes their dialogue with a zinger, "Do you think Jonathan's blame issues are deep enough to lead him to murder?"

Sue is shaken. She really never considered that possibility. She mutters, "Perhaps." Sullivan thanks her for her cooperation and leaves.

CHAPTER TWENTY-ONE

Jack Martini starts down the list of potential witnesses for the plaintiffs in their civil case against the Carusos and their company. As agreed upon with the Andersons and Attorney Cotter, he is to contact the paternal grandmother of Chip, Roberta Caruso, and halfheartedly request an interview with her regarding Chip. Hopefully, she will decline his invitation. Then, as planned, Jack will move on to his real desired witness, Chip's maternal grandmother, Marie Roselli, and push real hard for an interview.

Jack calls the elder Caruso's home in Brooklyn and asks to speak to Mrs. Roberta Caruso. In a few minutes, she comes on the line, and Jack begins, "Good afternoon, Mrs. Caruso, my name is Jack Martini. I'm calling about your grandson, Chip. We're trying to develop a profile of him, and we think you could help. It'll only take an hour or so, and I can come to your home to meet you and do the interview."

Roberta responds, "What can I possibly tell you about Chip that you don't already know? He's a nice kid and we love him. I can't add much more than that."

Jack, with a bit of a sly grin on his face, concludes their conversation, "Well, thanks anyway for talking with me. Have a nice day."

Moving right along, Jack now calls the Roselli household and gets right through to Marie, Chip's maternal grandmother. He introduces himself and explains his mission. After answering several of her questions, she agrees to see him at her home. They set the date and the time, and Jack hangs up.

Jack Martini identifies himself to Mrs. Maria Roselli, Carmella Caruso's mother and Chip's grandmother, at the front door of her beautiful home in Bergenfield, New Jersey. Once inside and seated, he opens with an explanation for their get-together, "As you know, Chip, your grandson, was involved in an automobile accident back in May. We're trying to develop a better understanding of what kind of a young man he is. We thought that you could fill in some of the blanks for us."

"If you don't mind, I'm going to record our conversation so I don't miss any of your points. My memory is not what it used to be."

She agrees and he continues, "Tell me about Chip as a youngster."

Grandma Marie responds, "Chip was always a beautiful, spirited child. When he got old enough, he became involved in sports like basketball and baseball. We just loved him to pieces."

Suddenly, she seems to sense that something is up and asks, "Is Chip in trouble?"

Jack responds, "Not exactly, but that auto accident I mentioned before ended up costing the life of a young girl in the other car." "Oh, that's terrible," sighs Grandma Marie. "I'll say a prayer for her tonight."

Jack continues, "We already know a lot about the girl's mother who was driving the other car, but we need to know more about Chip. Can you think of anything that might help us better understand your grandson?"

Marie answers, "Well, he always had a lot of friends. They were a harem-scarem kind of crowd. They got together a lot through high school and into college. By the way, how did the auto accident happen?"

Jack replies, "There's evidence that drinking was involved."

Apparently shocked by that statement, Marie mutters, "I had hoped that his drinking days were over."

Jack, pleased with the direction of their conversation, encourages her to go on, "Was drinking an issue for Chip in high school?"

She nods and replies, "Once Chip and his gang got their driving licenses, drinking seemed to have begun. There were a lot of scrapes with the authorities involving drinking and foolish behavior. I remember my daughter Carmella, Chip's mother, telling me about Chip being dumped at her front door on the night of the junior prom. He was drunk as a skunk and could hardly walk. He threw up on her brand-new living room carpeting. Carmella couldn't believe her precious son could do such a thing. Once Chip graduated from high school and was accepted into Fordham

University, we all thought that the strict Jesuit fathers at Fordham would straighten him out. But we were wrong."

She goes on, "In his sophomore year, after many warnings for drinking and misbehaving, the resident director of his dorm reported him to the dean of students. He was assigned to the Center for Drug and Alcohol Addiction for counseling."

"Nothing seemed to work. Somehow he managed to talk himself out of other scrapes and avoided being thrown out of school."

"Thank you so much for your insights. I know Chip a lot better now," responds Jack as he packs up and prepares to leave her home.

~

A low ground-hugging fog has settled over the eastern tip of Long Island. The combination of the misty fog and the dearth of moonlight create a dark inky atmosphere in the town of North Woodlane that early Tuesday morning.

No one notices a vehicle slowly inching along Professor Anderson's tree-lined street. Several houses up from his, the vehicle stops by the curb. A shadowy figure exits the vehicle, carrying a small box. The slinking figure slowly approaches the professor's driveway and his parked Cadillac.

Four dull metal railroad spikes are removed from the box and each is carefully set at a slight angle into the car's tires.

Once all the spikes are set, the stranger quietly returns to his vehicle and departs the area.

~

After breakfast, Professor Anderson heads out to his car for an uneventful jaunt over to the campus. By now, the fog has dissipated, and the sun has risen.

He slides into the driver's seat and starts his car.

As he starts to back out of his driveway, he instantly hears a chorus of whushes and thumps as his tires are all punctured. He leaps from his car to find out what just happened.

Bending down at the driver's side front tire, he notices its flattened state and the head of a spike protruding from the tire. Checking, he finds the other tires in a like condition.

He lets out an audible "bitch" and goes back into his house to call AAA for a most unusual emergency road-service request.

~

PI Martini visits the Last Call to see if he can develop a better understanding of Chip Caruso's drinking proclivity. He enters the well-appointed sports bar, identifies himself, and asks to speak with the owner or manager. He is directed to the rear office of Tom Wendell, the manager.

Martini requests a few minutes of his time to discuss one of his customers, Chip Caruso. Wendell acknowledges his acquaintance with Chip and invites Martini to join him at a side table.

Martini opens, "I'm trying to fill in some of the details that occurred back in May when Chip was involved in that tragic auto accident. Do you think you can help me?"

"I'll try my best," replies Wendell.

"Let's start with that tragic day. Were you around that day?" asks Martini. Wendell nods and adds, "It was a busy day, so I was helping out with the bartending and table waiting."

Martini continues, "Do you recall Chip Caruso and his friends on that particular day?" "Oh yes!" replies Wendell. "They would have been hard to forget. They all sat over in the corner by our sixty-inch high-definition television set, watching and cheering for the Yankees. They were playing the dreaded Boston Red Sox. I think there were seven or eight of them and the Caruso kid seemed to be the leader."

Martini interjects, "What were they drinking?"

"I recall that we were serving them pitchers of beer. Everyone seemed to be drinking the beer except for Chip. He was drinking Cuba Libres—that's Bacardi Gold with Coca-Cola in a tall glass. The strange thing I noticed about that drink was that Chip would scoop out three or four ice cubes every time he was served a fresh cocktail. He had a pocket flask on him and when he took out the ice cubes, he added what I assumed was rum to his glass. He was drinking real potent drinks that day."

"What kind of condition was he in when he got ready to leave?" asks Martini.

Wendell recounts how he had cut Chip off when he became loud and boisterous. He continues, "That didn't totally stop him since he had his private rum supply. At around nine o'clock, I suggested that one of his buddies call a cab for him. He was unsteady on his feet at that point. He vehemently refused the offers of assistance and left. When he was gone, I heard several of his friends commenting on how those double shots of rum really got to him."

Martini thanks Wendell for his forthrightness, shakes his hand, and exits the Last Call. He is very pleased with this interview and its disclosures.

On his way back to his office, he reviews his progress to date and feels that the time is right to contact the Carusos' private investigator, Coco Crandell, and set up a meeting. While they are each engaged by opposing factions, perhaps there is some common ground to expose. It's worth a shot, thinks Martini.

Martini makes contact with Coco Crandel. They agree to meet at Coco's office the next day at two o'clock.

They meet and exchange greetings. Coco invites Martini to have a seat. Martini opens their dialogue with "Well, we've both been chasing a multiple of leads in various cases. There has to be some areas where we both have little self-interest that we can talk freely about them." Coco agrees and asks, "Curiosity question. Why have the Andersons engaged your services?" Martini replies that there are strange things going on in their circle that they would like to resolve. For example, there have been death threats and accusations of poisoning aimed their way. Coco seems satisfied with his explanation and goes on, "Did you know about our involvement with the Mafia?"

Martini's eyes sparkle as he responds, "No, I'm not aware of any Mafia ties to any of the areas of my investigation. Tell me about it."

Coco responds, "Caruso Construction Company ended up bidding against a Mafia-controlled construction company on several municipal construction bids. Caruso Construction exposed the Mafia company's falsified minority ownership claim and that company lost out on all of their bids. After that, things started to happen. Mr. Caruso's daughter's pet cat was stolen and returned dead at a birthday party. A dead fish arrived at Mr. Caruso's desk; the Caruso's summer home was vandalized. And worst of all, the brake lines on Mr. Caruso's classic '54 Chevy Impala were cut. Fortunately, Mr. Caruso wasn't injured when his car collided with another car."

Martini is astounded at Coco's revelations and responds, "Wow. I don't see much of a connection between the Mafia and everything else that's going on."

Coco agrees. "And by the way, were you aware of the Carusos' neighbor being poisoned by a toxic plant's seed powder?"

Martini responds, "No, I didn't know about the poisoning."

Realizing that they're really getting nowhere with this dialogue, Martini attempts to wrap up their discussion, "I don't know that we've solved any of the criminal matters before us, but at least, we've aired them. We can both be mindful of them as we go forward."

Coco agrees, "You're right. Let's keep in touch and see how it goes."

Martini and Coco shake hands and bid each other good luck and farewell.

~

Martini decides to contact the police officer who was at the scene of the car accident back in May. He tracks him down to his police station and calls him.

"Hello, Officer Baggins, I'm Jack Martini, a retired NYC police officer turned private investigator. I'm looking into a car accident you responded to in May. The two parties involved in the crash were Caruso and Anderson. Could you review your files on this accident and then sit down with me for a few minutes to answer a few questions?"

Baggins agrees to help Martini out. They decide to meet at Baggins's station house the following day at the end of his day shift at four o'clock.

Upon meeting, there is instant chemistry between the two men. There wasn't a lot Martini wanted to ask Baggins. He went right to the heart of the matter, "How drunk was Chip Caruso that night?"

Baggins responds, "There was little doubt of his intoxication. He was wobbly, and his language was a bit garbled. I knew he would flunk the BAT test. And he did."

Martini asks, "Can you think of anything else I should know about him that evening?"

Baggins responds in the negative. Martini thanks him and they part ways.

~

Martini arranges with Attorney Cotter to meet at his office at six o'clock so Martini can bring him up-to-date on his very successful activities.

That evening, Martini details Cotter on his numerous meetings and interviews. Cotter is quite impressed with Martini's results. He is particularly moved by Martini's documentation of Chip Caruso's drinking problems.

Cotter is also enamored with the details of the other serious issues facing the Caruso family. The tangential matters should divert some of their attention away from their lawsuit.

CHAPTER TWENTY-TWO

That evening, as Coco is going over the details of his day, he particularly reflects on his conversation with the Andersons' private investigator, Jack Martini.

As expected, Martini, being a sharp investigator, was cagey; he didn't reveal any state secrets or tip the Anderson's game plan.

Coco didn't disclose to Martini what he had uncovered about Chip Caruso's actions over the past few months. Nor did he inform Charles Caruso of his shocking revelations regarding Chip.

~

As a follow-up on his investigation of the break-in and vandalism of the Carusos' summer home in Stony Pines, Coco visits with Detective Ryan Kuhn of the Stony Pines Police Department.

Having met with Detective Kuhn earlier in their investigations of the Carusos' house intrusion and having subsequently developed a cop-to-retired-cop bonding, Coco smiles as he extends his hand to Detective Kuhn, "Good morning, Ryan, how are you today?"

Kuhn replies with a grin, "It's nice to see you again, Coco. What can I do for you today?"

"Just checking back on the Caruso house break-in and vandalism case. Anything turn up yet?" asks Coco.

"Well, just between us two girls, that case has been solved and closed," answers Kuhn.

He goes on, "Believe it or not but we were able to hang that one on Mr. Caruso's own son, Chip. It seems that he was quite upset with his father over a job issue so he perpetrated these criminal acts to get back at him. The kid confessed when confronted with the evidence we had accumulated. His company car was recognized at the summerhouse earlier in that day. His DNA was discovered on several of the shards from the shattered window panel in the kitchen door. Also, the house-watch people had been at the house that morning and had set the alarm when they left, the alarm wasn't set when Chip and his friends arrived that evening. He knew we had him dead to rights, and so he confessed."

"He will be appearing at night court later this week, I'll get you the exact date before you leave."

Coco is bedazzled by the news. That Chip would do such a heinous act against his own family, especially his father, floors him.

After a few moments of reflection, Coco says, "I sure didn't see that one coming at all. Now I'll have to figure out how and when to disclose this disturbing news to his father. In any case, I certainly appreciate your cooperation on this case. As I've said before, if there's ever anything I can do for you, just give me a call. Thanks a lot." They part.

~

Irene, feeling particularly upbeat, tells Sue that she is thinking of inviting Jonathan over to the house for lunch and a swim on Thursday afternoon. Sue quickly agrees. She thinks it's a grand idea since Jonathan now has his driver's license and his own car.

Pleased with Sue's response, Irene calls Jonathan at Sunnyvale Meadows. He is happy to hear her voice again. Irene invites him over on Thursday at noon for a light lunch and a swim with Sue and her. Jonathan jumps at the kind invitation.

"Thanks, I'd love to join you and Sue. With my own car, I can drive myself. All I need are some directions and a bathing suit. I'll pick one up this afternoon," concludes Jonathan.

Irene gives him directions to her house and asks, "Are you sure you're up to a trip like this?" Jonathan answers, "You bet."

"We'll be expecting you around noon on Thursday. See you then," concludes Irene.

She tells Sue that their pool party is all set for Thursday at noon.

~

After several extended meetings with his private investigator, Jack Martini, Attorney Cotter decides to call an evening meeting of all the parties, including Irene Anderson and Professor Randolph Anderson for Thursday at seven o'clock in his office.

All the parties arrive on time and Attorney Cotter welcomes them and begins, "Since we last got together, Jack has been very busy interviewing potential witnesses for our side. I would like to have Jack review these interviews with you along with his observations."

Jack Martini begins his presentation with his experience with Chip Caruso's grandmothers, "As Raymond suggested, Chip's maternal grandmother, Marie Roselli, proved to be more incisive and family oriented than his paternal grandmother, Roberta Caruso. She couldn't be bothered talking with me about her extended family."

He goes on, "Mrs. Roselli obviously is involved in her grandchildren's lives. This is particularly true when it comes to Chip, her first and most favorite grandson. She was so enamored with him that she disclosed some interesting and very useful information regarding Chip's growing up years and his long-term affection for alcohol."

Cotter interjects, "Fascinating, Jack. Go on."

Jack continues, "Chip has always been popular with his schoolmates. In fact, he's more like the leader of the pack. Once driver licenses and automobiles became available to them in high school, drinking really entered their social equation. Even though they were all well below the legal drinking age, they managed to get their hands on illegal beer and liquor.

"He kept his drinking affinity secret from his parents who trusted him without question until the night of his junior prom in high school. Chip was dropped off at his home in the wee hours of that prom night. He staggered into his house and proceeded to throw up on his mother's brand-new living room carpeting. That set off the parental-alcohol-alert alarm.

"When he was accepted into Fordham University, the Carusos thought that the strict discipline of the Jesuit priests would straighten him out. Actually, the opposite happened. He got into a group of swingers in his dorm and the drinking and bad behavior began. Chip was continually chastised by his dorm's resident director for repeated violations of the university's rules for proper dorm behavior.

"It got so bad that his resident director finally reported him to his parents and the dean of students for his repeated behavior violations. The dean had him assigned to the University's Center for Drug and Alcohol Counseling. They counseled him and monitored his dorm activity for the rest of his time at Fordham. Somehow he was able to cajole his way through the four years and graduate."

Jack concludes his report on Chip with an assessment, "His behavior sure boosts our case."

Attorney Cotter looks over at Irene and Randolph and remarks, "That's the kind of evidence we need to win negligence cases like ours."

Randolph opines, "Now I despise that kid even more."

Cotter continues, "Jack also managed to arrange for a meeting with a Tom Wendell, the manager of the Last Call, the sports bar where Chip and his friends were drinking on the day of the fatal car accident. Jack, please do go on."

Jack starts with "It seems that Tom Wendell was on duty that fateful day and actually helped out with table waiting to Chip's party. He informed me that everyone but Chip was drinking beer. He was drinking Bacardi rum and Coca-Cola. Every time he was served with a fresh drink, Chip would spoon out a number of ice cubes from his tall glass and fill it with a shot of additional rum out of a flask he carried in his back pocket.

His buddies saw that he was well on his way to total intoxication and around eight thirty that evening they started to encourage him to call it a night and take a cab home. Chip adamantly refused their offers of assistance, and with a slight stagger, he made it out to his father's Lexus and took off.

"The combination of the testimony of his maternal grandmother and Tom Wendell certainly seems to prove that Chip Caruso has a serious drinking problem and shouldn't be driving a car," Martini concludes.

Cotter adds, "You're right about that, but in itself it doesn't completely make our case. The insurance companies and the New York State Judiciary System rely greatly on the principle of pure comparative fault. This means that if an injured person is partially at fault for causing his own injuries, his damages are reduced by the percentage of his perceived fault. That's why fault determination is so critical to the winning of our case.

"If we can prove that Chip Caruso and in turn the Caruso family and company are primarily responsible for the fatal automobile accident, our case is strengthened.

"So you can be sure that their attorneys and their insurance carrier will be hell-bent to minimize Chip Caruso's contributory negligence while ratcheting up our fault responsibility."

Both Randolph and Irene are in awe of the presentations of both Cotter and Martini. Cotter assures them the case is moving along at a rapid pace. He says that he will be expecting a flood of legal motions by the opposing counsel once the lawsuit is filed and served on the Carusos. He concludes this review session with handshakes all around.

~

Detective Sullivan of the Nassau County Homicide Division places a call to Coco Crandel and arranges for a get-together at Sullivan's office in Garden City at two o'clock next Tuesday afternoon.

Coco arrives on schedule and walks into Sullivan's cluttered office. They introduce each other and sit down. Sullivan settles into his desk chair and Coco sits in a chair in front of Sullivan's desk.

Sullivan opens with "I understand you've been working on the possible homicide of Mrs. Janet Zook, I could use some help on that case. Since the poisoning apparently occurred in Mrs. Caruso's garden next to her home in Harborport, the Carusos have much to answer for. I will be interviewing Mr. and Mrs. Caruso shortly, but before I do, I have a few key questions for you. Are you game?"

Coco is responsive and replies with a smile, "I'm your witness, counselor."

Sullivan starts with "Do you have a suspicion as to who could have caused most of the problems encountered by your clients, the Carusos, since the fatal car crash?"

Coco responds, "Believe it or not, I really don't have a viable suspect in mind at this time. The most obvious suspect seems to be Professor Randolph Anderson. He has publically expressed his desire to kill the young Caruso. Remember, it was his daughter who died as a result of an automobile accident with the Carusos' car. I'd say the only other possible suspect would be Irene Anderson. She is the mother of that little girl, and she was driving the other car involved in that accident. She has a strong motive to do harm to the Carusos even though it's her husband whom she mostly blames for their daughter's death."

Sullivan wasn't expecting much more from Coco. He does work for the Carusos. Sullivan thanks Coco for coming in and talking with him. Coco acknowledges Sullivan's appreciation, shakes his hand, and leaves.

Sullivan's next visit is with Mrs. Carmella Caruso. He calls her and sets up a convenient time for both of them to meet at her home.

Carmela responds to the doorbell ring and greets Detective Sullivan at the door. She leads him into her sitting room where they can sit across from each other in two plush chairs.

He begins, "This whole poisoning episode seems to have started when you asked Mrs. Zook to actually do some weeding in your garden when you and your family were away for several days."

Carmella nods affirmatively. Sullivan goes on, "But why was weeding so essential when you were only going to be away for a couple of days?"

Carmella responds, "I'm just obsessed with my flower garden. I just can't allow any weeds to germinate and contaminate my pristine garden. You've got to pluck them out when they first pop up."

Sullivan follows up with "Do you have any idea how the poison got into the soil in your garden?" Carmella quickly replies, "No idea. I never use anything but a branded fertilizer. But you know, my garden is always open to the public, so who knows?"

And, as a closing inquiry, Sullivan asks Carmella the "sixty-four-dollar question," "You know that you probably were the intended victim for that poison powder in your garden. Can you think of anyone who despised you or your family so much that they would go to such extremes? This certainly appears to be a case of murder by accident."

Carmella takes pause after that zinger and finally responds, "I really never thought of that possibility. Gosh, I really can't think of anyone who would wish me or my family such harm."

Sullivan thanks her for her candid opinions and excuses himself and leaves.

CHAPTER TWENTY-THREE

Irene makes an appointment with Dr. Jerome Jensen, her long-term personal physician, to discuss a scary new physical condition that has recently gripped her.

Dr. Jensen greets her and asks what concerns her. Irene explains that in the past few weeks, she has been having terrible nightmares and she doesn't know how to stop them.

After checking Irene's blood pressure and pulse, Dr. Jensen asks a few preliminary questions, "After you fall asleep, how long does it take before you have an episode?" Irene answers, "They usually occur shortly after I fall asleep. I don't ever remember what these nightmares are about."

Dr. Jensen continues his probing for more clues to Irene's nighttime trauma.

"Is your life more stressful now than it was when you first had to deal with the loss of your daughter?"

"Oh yes," responds Irene. "Then I was dealing with a loved one with compassion. Now I've become a wretched individual, I'm filled with animosity and anger toward my husband. He could have prevented that fatal crash. And I have similar feelings for that young drunken punk who caused the accident. I'm totally consumed with loathing."

"Well, Irene" continues Dr. Jensen, "I think your problem isn't nightmares. They usually occur later in one's sleep cycle. And most people have at least partial recall of the nightmare. In your case, I believe we're dealing with a condition known as a night terror or *pavor nocturnes* in medical jargon. This condition is trauma based rather than genetic. There are some pharmacological assists I can prescribe, or we can pursue treatment through psychotherapy. What do you prefer?"

Irene quickly replies, "I can't possibly get involved in serious therapy at this time. Let's try the drug approach." She's afraid that unless they take immediate steps to lessen her almost nightly attacks, they might intensify and cause physical harm.

Dr. Jensen writes out a prescription form for twenty milligrams of Nocturlyn Dx taken daily at bedtime. He adds, "Let's see how you react to this modest dosage. Make an appointment for a follow-up visit in thirty days unless you experience complications that are troublesome."

Irene thanks him and heads out to his reception area.

~

Thursday turns out to be a perfect day for dining alfresco, followed by a refreshing dip in Irene's kidney-shaped pool. The temperature is comfortable, and the sky is cloudless.

At about ten minutes to twelve, Jonathan pulls into Irene's driveway in his dream car.

He can hardly contain himself. He hops out of his snappy-looking Saturn Vue and skips up the walk to her front door. Irene answers his gentle knock and opens the door. She greets him with a firm hug and a kiss.

"Jonathan, it's so good to see you again. Did you have any trouble with my driving directions?" Irene asks.

"No," responds Jonathan. "Your directions were perfect. Now let me show you and Sue my new car."

Irene calls for Sue to join her in viewing Jonathan's new car. Sue comes rushing out and greets Jonathan.

He leads them out to his car and asks, "What do you think of it? It's a beauty, isn't it?"

The oohs and aahs of Irene and Sue say it all.

The happy trio move through Irene's gorgeous interior and out to her covered terrace where lunch and Alfie are waiting for them. After introducing Jonathan to Alfie, they sit at a round table and begin to partake. Their small talk during lunch is lively and very familiar. Jonathan is enamored with Alfie.

After their meal, they change into their bathing attire and gather at poolside. It occurs to Irene that Jonathan probably doesn't know how to swim and might be terrified at the sight of the deep pool. She goes to her pool shed and brings out an adult-sized inflated tube for him to use. Jonathan appreciates her gesture and gleefully gets into the tube. He carefully enters the pool. He loves it and is soon floating all around the pool.

As Jonathan floats over to the far end of the pool, he notices the end of an electrical extension cord jutting out from the pool's landscaping. He calls it to Irene's attention, "Irene, isn't that cord dangerous so close to the water? Back at Sunnyvale, they're always warning us about the dangers of water and electricity."

Irene quickly reassures him, "That extension cord isn't plugged in; don't worry, we're safe."

Sue nods her head knowingly.

Jonathan is so pleased to be in a swimming pool for the first time in his life. He'll never forget this special moment.

The afternoon rolls on much too fast for these happy campers. Their problems all seem to fade away for the nonce. Soon it's time to say good-bye.

Jonathan thanks the ladies for a great afternoon together. He ends with "We'll have to do this again sometime soon."

They hug and kiss and Jonathan pops into his joy mobile and sets off for Sunnyvale.

~

Continuing his investigation, Detective Sullivan makes arrangements to have Chip Caruso come into his office after work hours. Sullivan would like to interview him regarding the various episodes connected to the Caruso family. Chip agrees and appears after work on Wednesday.

"Thank you for coming in," starts Sullivan. "I just have a few questions for you this afternoon. Let's get started. I'm sure you're familiar with all the players in this human tug-of-war that's going on. First off, there are the parents of the young girl killed as a result of the collision of your car and theirs back in May. I'm, of course, referring to the Andersons, Randolph, and Irene. Any thoughts about the involvement of either or both of them in what's been going on?"

Chip hesitatingly begins with "I know Mrs. Anderson was driving the other car involved in the crash. The official accident report states that she was distracted by a disturbing cell phone call right before the crash. She apparently was also speeding, and she ran a red light. She must be very upset and could be trying to avenge her daughter's death by attacking my family."

Sullivan interjects, "And what about her husband, Professor Anderson?"

Chip responds, "He seems to be more vengeful than his wife. I remember going to their daughter's funeral services and running into him. He came over to me and knocked me down. He yelled out loud that he will kill me. He really scared me. I don't know anything else about him."

"Well, Chip, let me ask you this," continues Sullivan. "Who do you think cut your father's brake lines and who do you think vandalized your parents' summer home?"

Chip appears bewildered and mutters, "I have no idea."

Sullivan thanks him for meeting with him and sends him off.

Charles Caruso Sr. is next on Sullivan's interview list. He calls him at his office and explains that he would like to get his take on various elements of his investigation in this very complicated case. Sullivan offers, as a professional courtesy, to drive over to Caruso's office for the interview.

Promptly at the designated time, Sullivan is ushered into Charles's office. They introduce each other and Sullivan begins, "Do you have any strong suspicions on who has been causing your family so much grief over recent months?"

Charles thinks for a moment and responds, "Detective Sullivan, I've asked myself that very same question almost every night, and to tell you the truth, I don't have an answer. There are lots of involved parties but no solid suspects."

Sullivan follows up with "Does that also go for the poisoning of your neighbor and the cutting of your brake lines?"

"Yes," responds Charles. "The poisoning is beyond my comprehension. How could anyone be so evil? Regarding my cut brake lines, the local police department hasn't turned up a clue as yet. We all assume that the brake lines were severed right here in our rear parking lot. We haven't a positive ID of the culprit, except that he probably has bright blond hair. And, of course, Professor Randolph Anderson fits that description, so I guess that could make him a person of interest."

Sullivan nods his head and adds, "Any further thoughts on the involvement of the Mafia?"

Charles frowns and replies, "I think the timing of our entanglement with the mob was coincidental. We had a business problem with Tony Bianco's construction company around the same time as all the other things were going on. I just don't see any Mafia connection with everything else."

Sullivan rises and thanks Charles for his cooperation and insight. They shake hands and Sullivan leaves.

Sullivan is now prepared to tackle his most formidable witness yet, Professor Randolph Anderson. He has his assistant arrange for Anderson to meet with Sullivan in his office at a convenient time for Anderson.

Anderson shows up on schedule and is escorted into one of the DA's interrogation rooms. Sullivan soon joins him in the room and introduces himself.

"Professor Anderson, I'm investigating numerous facets of what appears to be a conspiracy against the Caruso family. I'd like to get your input on some of the key elements of the case. Since one significant element is the poisoning of the Carusos' neighbor, we're dealing with a possible homicide case here. Accordingly I would like your permission to tape our interview. I'll have the entire tape transcribed and send you a complete unabridged copy for your records. Does that suit you, Professor?"

Anderson answers, "No problem."

Sullivan then reads him his Miranda rights and asks him, "Do you understand these rights?"

Anderson answers in the affirmative.

"Okay, let's get started. Did you ever order poisonous rosary pea plants from a grower in Florida?"

Anderson nods yes. Sullivan adds, "I take your nod as a yes. What did you do with those plants?"

Anderson explains, "I ordered them for a special summer course I was going to teach at Strafford College on toxins in the environment. I ground up the plants' seeds into a powder in my home workshop and placed the powder into six or seven sealed plastic bags. I took about half of the bags to school to demonstrate how harmless the toxic powder appeared. I then discarded those bags in the college's pharmaceutical lab's toxic waste container."

Sullivan asks a follow-up question, "What happened to the bags you left at your home workshop?"

Anderson answers, "I labeled them as toxic and put them in a small box which I placed in my workbench cabinet."

"Moving to another subject," Sullivan inquires, "Have you ever been to the Carusos' house in Harborport?"

Anderson, appearing a bit on edge, promptly responds, "No, never!"

That response astounds Sullivan, who clearly recalls Investigator Thompson's transitional report that included the Carusos' gatehouse guard's record of the Andersons passing through the gates. He lets that point go by at this point and moves on.

"How about the Caruso Construction Company headquarters building? Have you been there?"

"Yes," answers Anderson. "I think it was in early June. I drove out there to see it on a lark."

Sullivan concludes the interrogation with a pleasantry, "Thank you for coming in. I'll forward you a copy of the transcript as soon as it is completed."

Anderson gets up from the conference table, sighs silently, and departs.

CHAPTER TWENTY-FOUR

At 10:52 AM on November 3, Marshal Harold Nelson rings the doorbell at the residence of the Carusos. When Carmella opens the door, he serves her with court papers of a lawsuit filed by Randolph C. Anderson and Irene G. Anderson in the wrongful death of their daughter, Erin Anne Anderson. Carmella signs for the package and shuts the door.

She opens the package and reviews the first few pages to better understand the situation and to be able to communicate with her husband, Charles, about it:

UNITED STATES DISTRICT COURT
NASSAU AND SUFFOLK COUNTIES, NEW YORK

RANDOLPH C. ANDERSON and	)
IRENE G. ANDERSON	)
Plaintiffs,	) **CIVIL NO. 63448**

vs.	**)**
CHARLES A. CARUSSO, CARMELLA J. CARUSO,	**) COMPLAINT FOR**
CHARLES A. CARUSSO, JR.	**) WRONGFUL DEATH**
And	**)**
CARUSO CONSTRUCTION COMPANY, INC.	**)**
Defendants.	**)**

Plaintiffs, RANDOLPH C. ANDERSON and

IRENE G. ANDERSON, alleges

COMPLAINT AND ELECTION OF JURY TRIAL

I. PARTIES

Randolph C. Anderson and Irene G. Anderson, Plaintiffs, by and through their undersigned attorney bring suit against the afore cited Defendants as follows:

Randolph C. Anderson and Irene G. Anderson are married and the parents of the decedent, Erin Anne Anderson. They both reside in Nassau County, New York.

Other than the stated Plaintiffs, there are no other persons entitled to recover damages for the wrongful death of the decedent.

Defendants Charles A. Caruso Sr. and Carmella J. Caruso both reside in Nassau County, New York.

Caruso Construction Company, Inc. is a corporation organized and existing under the laws of the State of New York. Its primary place of business is located in Nassau County, New York. They are general contractors who are engaged in the design, development and construction of commercial and municipal properties.

On May 14, 2010, Erin Anne Anderson was picked up from a dance lesson by her mother at approximately 10:10 PM in Garden City.

On or about 9:50 PM on May 14, 2010, Charles A. Caruso Jr. left The Last Call, a sports bar after an afternoon of drinking with friends.

II. JURISDICTION

Plaintiffs bring this action pursuant to New York State Constitution Article 1, S16, which made pecuniary recovery inviolate. Further, the Estate Powers and Trust Law (EPTL), Article 5, Part 4, EPTL 213-217 provides that punitive damages, designed to punish the Defendants in case of recklessness or depravity are allowed.

COUNT 1—RECKLESSNESS

At approximately 10:20 PM on May 14, 2010, Charles A. Caruso Jr. recklessly and at excessive speed drove a passenger car owned and registered by Caruso Construction Company into the automobile of Plaintiff Irene G. Anderson causing the subsequent death of her daughter, Erin Anne Anderson on May 20, 2010. A certified death certificate is appended herewith.

Charles A. Caruso Jr. has a long history of alcohol abuse and reckless behavior. His drinking problems began in high school and continued into college on an elevated level. His dorm's resident assistant cited him often for drunken behavior. In his junior year, after a night of partying, Charles set off a fire alarm on his floor causing panic among his dorm mates. The Dean of Students severely reprimanded him and assigned him to the Substance Abuse Counseling Program for prolonged help. Knowing he had an alcohol problem, Charles A. Caruso Jr. should not have been drinking in the early afternoon of May 14, 2010. Evidencing his reckless mentality, he rebuffed his friends' offers to drive him home that afternoon.

Through the collective and willful negligence on the part of all the Defendants, the wrongful death of Erin Anne Anderson was precipitated.

WHEREFORE, Plaintiffs demand judgment against Charles A. Caruso Sr. and Carmella J. Caruso, Defendants, in the amount of Five Hundred Thousand Dollars ($500,000.00) in compensation and punitory damages plus interest and costs.

COUNT 2—PERSONAL NEGLIGENCE

Knowing of Charles A. Caruso's propensity to overindulge in alcohol and his date to meet with his college friends for drinks on May 14, 2010, neither Charles A. Caruso Sr. nor Carmella J. Caruso, Defendants, should have permitted the use of any automobile by Charles A. Caruso Jr. Their negligence greatly contributed to the automobile accident that caused the death of Erin Anne Anderson.

WHEREFORE, Plaintiffs demand judgment against Charles A. Caruso Sr. and Carmella J. Caruso, Defendants, in the amount of Five Hundred Thousand Dollars ($500,000.00) in compensation and punitory damages plus interest and costs.

COUNT 3—CORPORATE NEGLIGENCE

Plaintiffs re-allege and incorporate herein the allegations cited in paragraphs 1 through 10 of this Complaint.

As a direct and proximate result of the Defendant's negligence, Erin Anne Anderson suffered a premature death. Plaintiffs Randolph C. Anderson and Irene G. Anderson, surviving parents of Erin Anne Anderson, sustained pecuniary loss, mutual anguish, emotional pain and suffering, loss of society, loss of companionship and loss of endearment and affection.

WHEREFORE, Plaintiffs Randolph C. Anderson and Irene G. Anderson, sole surviving parents of Erin Anne Anderson, demand judgment against Charles A. Caruso Sr. and Carmella J. Caruso, Defendants, in the amount of Five Hundred Thousand Dollars ($500,000.00) in compensation and punitory damages plus interest and costs.

DATED this *third* day of *November, 2010*

RAYMOND J. COTTER LAW OFFICE

____

RAYMOND J. COTTER, NYSBA #46588
Counsel for Plaintiffs

Carmella is stunned by the tone of the document and the incredible money demands. She calls her husband at his office and describes the lawsuit to him. As usual, Charles seems unflustered by the news and tells Carmella that he will be home in about an hour to deal with it.

After completing his call with Carmella, he places a call to his law firm and asks for Donald Langsford. Almost immediately, Donald picks up the call. “Good afternoon, Charles. How can I be of help to you today?”

Charles responds, “We were just served with a lawsuit by the parents of that young girl who died as a result of that accident that you helped Chip with. They’ve named me, Carmella, Chip and our company as codefendants.”

“Okay, we’ll have to get on this as soon as possible. When can you come in? You name the time.”

“I can be there in an hour,” Charles offers. “See you then,” Charles responds and hangs up and heads home.

Charles picks up the papers and is off to Langsford’s office.

~

Upon arriving at the law offices, Charles is ushered to Langsford’s office. After handshakes, they get down to business. Donald has his secretary make an extra copy of the citation, so they can review the details together.

First off, Donald notes that they are demanding a jury trial. He adds, “Jurors are much more sympathetic to plaintiffs, especially when the death of a young child is involved. We’ll have to work on that issue. Judges are much more impartial and rely more on the facts of a case rather than the emotional issues.”

Donald Langsford continues, “They very cleverly included your company as a defendant. This helps them cloud the main issue of the case and provide any jury with yet another reason to side with the heartbroken parents of the lost child. We will have to develop a strategy to position that matter as a side issue and not the main focus of the case. A first reading of this citation clearly outlines their strategy—focus on the drinking habits of Chip. They can claim what they want, but they will have to substantiate all of their allegations. That will be difficult for them.”

Donald continues, “We will have to see exactly how strong they feel about the last few allegations in which you and Carmella are accused with parental negligence while you are further charged with negligence for allowing Chip to drive a company car knowing of his drinking affection.”

He concludes with "I'll get our civil litigation team on this right away. And we'll notify your corporate and personal liability carriers and get their input on how to move forward. After conferencing with your insurance companies, we'll develop the required response to this lawsuit. I'll call you when it's ready for review and signing."

Charles rises and says, "Somehow things never seem like doomsday when I get a chance to talk with you about them. Thank you." Charles leaves.

~

Irene decides that Jonathan needs some more up-to-date clothing. She heads over to Macy's department store in the Central Island Mall. Her selections of shirts, slacks, shoes, and jacket are identical to what she used to buy for Randolph. And she assumes that the twins are the same size when it comes to clothing and shoes.

With this new stylish wardrobe, Jonathan will really resemble his twin brother, Randolph. Of course Jonathan won't realize he's now a dead ringer for Randolph, especially with his new longer blond tresses.

Rather than presenting his new outfits in person and possibly face rejection, Irene has Macy's send the packages directly to Jonathan at Sunnyvale Meadows along with a cheerful note of thanks from Irene for being such a good friend during these trying days.

CHAPTER TWENTY-FIVE

"I hope someone is getting the message. As Cain proclaimed after murdering his brother, Abel, 'Am I my brother's keeper?' We all have felt the tragic loss of a beautiful young soul through sheer negligence; vengeance is demanded. Whose brother is keeping this going?"

~

Jonathan decides to contact Sue to see if they could get together for lunch on one of her work days. He would like to keep their lunch date quiet, so it will only be between the two of them.

Jonathan calls Sue on her cell phone, and they agree to meet outside one of Sue's market assignments. It's set for noon on Friday at the Superfood Market store on Old County Road in Westbury.

Jonathan leaves Sunnyvale at ten o'clock; he doesn't want to chance being late. By eleven thirty, he is parked in front of the Superfood Market store. At twelve on the dot, Sue comes walking out of the store and sees Jonathan walking toward her. They meet and hug.

He asks her to pick out a quiet place where they can talk privately and have a bite to eat. Sue leads them to a pleasant café in the same shopping center.

Once seated and lunch ordered, Jonathan opens with "I suppose you're wondering what this is all about. Well, I just wanted to get your opinion on several matters, mostly pertaining to Irene."

He goes on, "It seems that lately she has been a bit on edge. When we talk on the telephone her voice often seems to waver. And another thing,

Irene seems to be intensifying her blame attacks on my brother Randolph. Have you noticed these changes?"

Sue is a little surprised at Jonathan's intuitive observations. She also has noticed some not-so-subtle changes in Irene's demeanor and attitudes lately. She replies, "Irene is my best friend, and I don't want to be talking behind her back. I think what we are talking about is quite different and not gossipy. It's for her own good."

Sue continues, "I don't know if it's due to her job or not, but she certainly is edgier lately. The other night I heard her having, I guess, a nightmare. She was screaming at Randolph. I couldn't hear what it was all about."

Jonathan adds, "I realize my brother has his flaws, but it almost seems too convenient to blame him for everything. For example, those stories about her almost-fatal carbon monoxide poisoning in the garage and then the electrical extension cord in the swimming pool. Someone else could have staged those incidents but so could have Irene. What do you think?"

Sue responds, "You know, I've had those same nagging doubts. What can we do?"

"I think we should just monitor her behavior and see if her condition worsens," replies Jonathan.

~

It's Saturday morning, the day of the big move. Chip's buddies arrive at the Caruso home in Harborport, ready for some manual labor. Soon the three young men are loading all of Chip's worldly possessions and the bedroom furniture his parents agreed to part with into Johnnie's new panel truck. By eleven o'clock, they're all packed up and ready for their trip to Rego Park.

Chip hugs and kisses his mother good-bye and follows the moving truck to his new home in his packed company car.

~

Charles Caruso arranges to have Coco Crandel join himself and his wife, Carmella, for a follow-up meeting on the Andersons' lawsuit at Donald Langsford's office. After reviewing the particulars of the prior meeting between Charles Caruso and himself, Donald announces that his team has prepared a response to the complaint that is ready for review, signing, and transmittal.

Once that matter was considered and executed, Donald announces that his office has received a list of prospective plaintiff's witnesses. It includes Irene Anderson, Officer Matt Baggins, and the manager of the Last Call, Tom Wendell.

Donald speaks, "Well that pretty much catches us up to speed on this matter."

Coco interrupts, "Excuse me. Donald. Could I make a significant comment at this time?" They all voice their approvals, and Coco continues.

"This is difficult for me to say. Charles, I didn't know how to tell you this. You know that major episode you experienced with your summer home in Stony Pines? Well, the local police department out there informed me last week that Chip confessed to that whole affair to get even with you over not hiring him when he graduated college. I'm sorry."

Charles and Carmella gasp in unison.

Carmella mutters "oh my God" while Charles proclaims, "I can't believe our own flesh and blood could turn on us like that. It's inconceivable." She starts sobbing.

~

When Charles and Carmella arrive home in Harborport, they check their mailbox and notice a letter from the Stony Pines Courts. It confirms the news that Coco had just passed on to them earlier.

CHAPTER TWENTY-SIX

Jonathan reflects on his meeting with Sue concerning Irene's erratic behavior and mood swings over the last few months. He decides he will develop an "Irene Journal." In his journal, he will record his various interactions with Irene and his observations regarding them.

One of his first entries involves one of the automobile trips he had with Irene early in their relationship. Irene had picked him up at Sunnyvale in the morning in maybe late May or early June, and they drove out to the Carusos' beautiful home on Long Island.

When they arrived at the Carusos' gated community, they were stopped at the gatehouse. Even though both of them technically were Andersons, he thought it strange at the time that Irene answered the guard's identification query with "We're Mr. and Mrs. Anderson."

When they drove up to the Carusos' house, Irene parked her car on the far right of the very wide driveway. She then asked him to walk over past the Carusos' three garages to their left and walk up to the front door and ring the Carusos' doorbell. If Mrs. Caruso answered the doorbell, he was to ask her if they could walk through her garden. He waited for a response, but none came, so he walked back over toward Irene's car.

She wasn't in the car; she had walked into the nearby garden. She was ready to exit the garden as he arrived. She had plenty of time to spread that poisonous powder around the garden. She didn't say anything at that point, but she did seem uptight. And why did she wear her shoulder bag into the garden if she was just looking around? And even stranger, why was she wearing gloves?

His next entries dealt with their conversations, live and telephone. Irene never seemed to miss an opportunity to criticize his brother and to blame him for all of her woes.

From the very beginning of their relationship, Irene always spoke poorly of her husband. Their first face-to-face occurred three or four weeks after her terrible automobile accident in which her poor daughter, Erin, was so seriously injured and eventually died. Irene was the driver of one of the cars involved; Chip Caruso, son of a wealthy Long Island businessman, drove the other car.

There was plenty of guilt to spread around. Irene was talking on her cell phone at the time of the accident and she ran a red light at the accident intersection. The kid, Chip, also had plenty to answer for. He had been drinking heavily just prior to the accident.

From the first time Irene and I spoke of the accident, she never assumed any responsibility for her actions; she blamed her husband, Randolph, for almost complete responsibility for the accident since he forgot to pick up Erin at her dance academy that fateful evening. He swore he was at a faculty meeting and couldn't leave. She knew that was all a pack of lies. And if he had left after Irene called to remind him, Erin wouldn't be lying in that hospital. Plus he drove a Cadillac Escalade, which she was sure would have withstood the side impact better than her much smaller and lighter Toyota RAV4.

Everyone, including the police, seemed to be determined to blame every negative action on Randolph. It seemed like he was always the most promising suspect. No one seemed to suspect Irene. After all, she is a woman and a mother. How could she even think about such horrible acts like poisoning Mrs. Caruso's neighbor? And how about kidnapping and killing the Carusos' family cat? And could you imagine a lady like Irene crawling under Mr. Caruso's car and cutting his brake lines? It's a lot easier to imagine Randolph doing something like that.

The police should investigate Irene as thoroughly as they did Randolph. I'm sure they would uncover some real damning evidence against sweet Irene.

As time wore on, Irene's regard for Randolph worsened to total hatred. This was reflected in her language. Her longtime friend, Sue Greene, also noticed the total erosion of Irene and Randolph's relationship. Irene got to a point where she never spoke well of Randolph.

And when Erin finally passed away, Irene's stance stiffened. She seemed to be seeking revenge for Erin's death.

Sue mentioned to me the two near-death episodes that happened at Irene's house. The first was the carbon monoxide gas buildup in her garage. Someone had propped cement blocks on the weather stripping of Irene's garage doors, disabling the electronic door controls. How convenient that Sue showed up on time that evening.

The other episode involved Irene's swimming pool. Sue was set to jump into the pool when she noticed a portable radio and electric cord at the bottom of the pool. Irene quickly ran over behind the pool's shrubbery and unplugged the extension cord, or so she claimed.

Sue and I are very suspicious of these two incidents. We both think Irene could have staged them to cast suspicion on Randolph.

CHAPTER TWENTY-SEVEN

As Detective James Sullivan starts building his case against Randolph Anderson, he realizes that much of the case is purely circumstantial. To present this case to the grand jury and obtain a true bill will require substantial, substantive evidence. He ponders the various elements of his case to date:

1. *Death of Janet Zook*. Professor Anderson has admitted that he did purchase quantities of the rosary pea plant, which produces the fatal poison, abrin, from its seeds. He explains that the purchase was made in conjunction with a toxicology course he was teaching this past summer at his college. The professor also admits that he did have some packets of the poison left over after the course was completed. If Sullivan can locate those deadly packets, it would be very helpful.
2. *The Cutting of the Brake Lines of Charles Caruso's Antique Car.* Again, he has no physical evidence to tie this crime to Anderson. Can he even place Anderson at the scene of the brake-line cutting?
3. *The Killing of the Caruso's Cat.* The only evidence he has in this episode is the cat's body, which didn't provide any prosecutionary evidence.
4. *The Two Attempts on Irene Anderson's Life.* The only evidence of these attempts is personal suspicions.

It becomes patently apparent to Detective Sullivan that Anderson has done a professional job in covering his tracks in these episodes. Sullivan decides that he must gain access to Anderson's current residence and recover any physical evidence he might find there to bolster his case and win an indictment. He proceeds to develop a detailed affidavit outlining his rationale for a comprehensive search of the professor's home.

Detective Sullivan's sworn affidavit is well received by the prosecutor's office and is promptly processed and approved. Following the DA's approval of the search warrant of Professor Randolph Anderson's home, the affidavit is presented to Judge George Fuller for his review and approval. Detective Sullivan is summoned to the judge's chamber and questioned at length on the need and justification for this particular search. Satisfied with Detective Sullivan's responses, Judge Fuller approves the request for a search warrant pertaining to the residence of Professor Randolph Anderson.

Detective Sullivan and two plainclothesmen arrive at the professor's home at ten o'clock in the morning the following Saturday. The professor answers his doorbell. Detective Sullivan introduces himself again to Anderson and then introduces his associates. The official search warrant is presented and explained to the professor. Surprisingly, he offers no resistance to the search. Most people in his position complain and try to avoid compliance with the warrant.

The three lawmen section the house into searchable areas and begin their searches. One of the officers searches the professor's makeshift lab and soon discovers three sealed and marked plastic packets of rosary-pea seeds. The packets are placed in a special zippered evidence bag, which is appropriately identified.

Detective Sullivan searches the professor's bedroom. After checking his bureau and armoire and finding nothing suspicious, he moves into the professor's walk-in double closet. He quickly surveys all the hanging apparel as well as items on the shelves above the hangers. Still nothing of interest. He then checks the professor's shoes, boots, and slippers and finds nothing consequential.

In the far corner of the closet, he notices two medium-sized cardboard boxes. One was already open and Sullivan soon realizes that it's the box that contains the professor's skiing gear and clothing. Nothing raises Sullivan's suspicions, but just on a hunch, he decides to dust the cellophane tape on both boxes for fingerprints. He uncovers two latent prints and files them in his evidence portfolio. He then moves on and cuts the sealed tape on the second box.

Once opened, Sullivan finds a series of large plastic Husky storage bags, one on top of the other. He removes each of these bags and examines them for their contents. Each holds a quantity of shirts, ties, sweaters, pajamas, shorts, and underwear. When he lifts the final bag from the box, he notices several additional items lying at the bottom of the box. Detective Sullivan lifts each item out of the box. The first item is a pair of black coveralls, the second item is a black baseball cap, and the third item is a pair of pronged wire cutters. The final item is a bejeweled cat collar. Finally, Sullivan surmises, "The smoking gun!"

He packs up the four items in separate evidence bags and comes downstairs to query his associates on their findings. The only important find is the packets of rosary-pea seeds which produce the poison, abrin. That's the poison that killed Janet Zook, Mrs. Caruso's neighbor. Sullivan's case is beginning to gel.

Detective Sullivan thanks the professor for his cooperation, and the three lawmen leave without disclosing the results of their search.

~

Back at his office, Detective Sullivan presents his new evidence to his superiors. They are pleased with this new development in what has been a difficult case to nail down. Sullivan gets the green light on preparing his case for presentation to the grand jury. The prosecutor's office appoints James Johnson as lead presenter before the grand jury.

Along with the incriminating physical evidence accumulated during the search of Professor Anderson's residence, they also have the firsthand testimony of Sue Greene, the Andersons' longtime friend and associate. She will convincingly argue that Randolph Anderson despised his wife so deeply that he made two known attempts on her life. And Sue Greene was present shortly after each attempt to confirm them and to hear Irene denounce her husband for such vile actions. The first attempt involved the placing of heavy cement blocks against Irene's garage doors so as to seal in the deadly carbon monoxide along with Irene in her garage. The second attempt involved a live electrical line in Irene's swimming pool.

Chip Caruso, the other driver involved in the auto accident that took the life of the Andersons' only child, will provide the final nail in Professor Anderson's coffin with his testimony about the violent confrontation by Professor Anderson at his daughter's funeral.

Sure enough, when ADA James Johnson presents his solid case to the grand jury, he convinces the panel that Randolph Anderson is indeed the vengeful killer of Janet Zook and the perpetrator of the other listed felonies.

Within an hour after Johnson completes his presentation before the grand jury, they deliver the requested indictment of Randolph Anderson.

Johnson orders the arrest of Randolph Anderson. He is charged with the voluntary manslaughter of Janet Zook and the attempted manslaughter of Charles Caruso as well the other listed felonies. An arrest warrant is issued and Randolph Anderson is soon located and arrested. His arraignment before Judge Folger is scheduled for Friday of the arresting week.

Randolph is astonished by the swift turn of events but confident in his innocence. He is released on bail since he is a first-time offender. Upon release, Randolph's first order of business is to secure counsel to defend him against these scurrilous charges. With the valued input of his colleague, Raymond J. Cotter, he settles on Charles B. Flynn, an experienced trial attorney. They meet to review the charges and his possible defenses. After days of close consultation with Counsel Flynn, the defense team is prepared and appears at Anderson's arraignment before Judge Folger. Randolph pleads not guilty to all the charges and a trial date two weeks subsequent is set.

~

Judge Folger gavels the start of the trial of the state of New York versus Randolph Anderson. The jury has been empanelled and is prepared to hear the case. Once the opposing counsels have presented their opening statements, the trial is ready to proceed. On behalf of the state, Counsel James Johnson begins with the most serious of the charges, the involuntary manslaughter of Janet Zook. He explains the lengths defendant Anderson went to in locating an out-of-state source of the identified exotic poison abrin and then in attempting to rationalize its purchase with his lame college course need for the physical poison. Johnson goes on to cite the motive for this crime is the defendant's intense hatred of the Caruso family rising from the car accident that killed his daughter.

He goes on to state that the intended victim of the poison plant powder was not Janet Zook but the mother of Chip Caruso, the driver of the other car in that fatal accident. Janet Zook was a next-door neighbor of Carmella Caruso and had volunteered to weed her garden for several days before she died. Anderson's attorney raises a series of objections to Johnson's pointed allegations but is overruled by Judge Folger. Following the judge's ruling, Johnson shows the packets of the poisonous seeds to the jury and states that they were found in Professor Anderson's workshop during their search.

Counsel Johnson moves on to the charge of cutting the brake lines of Charles Caruso' car. He enters into evidence, over defense counsel's objection, a sworn statement by Robert "Bobby" Quinn, a serviceman who is employed by King of Oil, a company that services cars in the rear parking lot of Mr. Caruso's company headquarters. In his statement, Robert Quinn alleges that he witnessed Randolph Anderson, attired in black coveralls and cap, similar to King of Oil's company uniform, carrying a pair of wire cutters near Mr. Caruso's vehicle.

Again, Anderson's attorney objected to the admittance of Quinn's statement, alleging it is hearsay testimony at best and filled with unfounded allegations. Once again, the defense is crestfallen; their objection is overruled.

Prosecutor Johnson then introduces the black coveralls and baseball cap that were found hidden in a sealed box in Professor Anderson's bedroom closet. And he follows them with the wire cutters also found hidden in the professor's bedroom closet.

His final exhibit is the bejeweled cat collar that was also found hidden in the professor's closet. He introduces a notarized statement signed by Charles Caruso that identifies the collar as having belonged to his daughter's pet cat, which was brutally strangled. Also attached to his statement is a signed copy of the sales receipt from the jewelry store where the original collar was purchased. He passes the sparkling cat collar among the jurors for their perusal and then asks them, "Just consider the depravity of an individual who could kidnap a young girl's favorite pet cat and strangle the helpless animal. And then, as if that wasn't horrific enough, return the dead animal in a birthday-gift box at the young girl's surprise ninth birthday party. What a psychopath. And he actually kept this beautiful collar as a trophy in his bedroom."

His last witness is Chip Caruso. As he walks toward the witness stand, his eyes catch those of Professor Anderson's. It almost seemed that actual sparks were flying between them for an instance. After being sworn in, Chip proceeds to describe the events that followed the automobile accident in which he was the other driver. He details how he, out of sorrow and remorse, attended the Andersons' young daughter's funeral and was accosted by the professor and shoved to the ground with the professor yelling at him, "I'll kill you."

Johnson asks his witness, "Were those the exact words he yelled?" "Yes," responds Chip, "Exactly."

Prosecutor Johnson announces that the prosecution rests. He thanks the jury for their attention and sits down. Judge Folger checks his wristwatch and announces, "It's getting late into the afternoon. We'll adjourn now and resume proceedings tomorrow morning at nine o'clock. At that time, the defense will present their case. Court dismissed."

The near-full gallery of spectators exit the courtroom in an orderly fashion. No one seems to notice the nattily dressed forty-year-old man wearing a beret, concealing his cropped blond locks.

CHAPTER TWENTY-EIGHT

Jonathan keeps an eye on Randolph's attorney, Charles Flynn, as he exits the courtroom. Flynn follows the circular stairway down one flight and enters Room 34, a private office. Jonathan follows him in. Flynn is somewhat shaken by Jonathan's sudden appearance.

Jonathan, sensing Flynn's uneasiness, extends his hand in friendship and announces, "Attorney Flynn, I'm Jonathan Anderson, Randolph's twin brother." Flynn, startled by this admission, timidly extends his hand to Jonathan and asks, "What can I do for you?"

Jonathan replies, "I think I can help you with your case." He removes his beret and Flynn is astonished at the likeness of Jonathan to his twin brother. He says, "Let's sit down and talk."

Flynn starts, "How can you help us with our case?"

Jonathan begins, "I've been developing a relatively close relationship over the past six months with Irene Anderson, Randolph's wife. Strictly as friends, mind you. Initially, she located me at a rest home where I've been residing and recovering from the trauma received many years ago in a swing set accident. Over the years, I've blamed my brother Randolph for causing the accident and my injuries. As my relationship with Irene grew over time, I assumed her staunch condemnation of Randolph for causing the auto wreck that eventually took her only child's life.

"In recent months, I've noticed a significant change in Irene's disposition. Her hatred of Randolph has intensified, she blames him for everything. Actually, I believe she set him up for several unsuccessful attempts on her life . . . and there's more.

"Several months back, I began to keep a personal journal of my interactions with Irene including several suspicions I developed about her activities." Jonathan presents the journal to Flynn who begins to eagerly thumb through it.

"This is fantastic. I believe that together we can successfully defend Randolph from these charges. I'll petition the court for a two-day delay in the presentation of the defense's case."

Attorney Flynn prepares a thorough but concise brief for submission to Judge Folger, requesting a two-day stay in the State's case against his client, Randolph Anderson.

Once completed, Flynn requests an immediate meeting with Judge Folger when he can present and plead his case for a two-day stay in the proceedings. Judge Folger reads through the brief and asks a few pertinent questions. Satisfied with the truthfulness and the importance of the appeal, the judge grants the two-day stay and the opportunity for Jonathan Anderson to testify on behalf of his brother, Randolph.

Two days later, Judge Folger once again calls his court to order. The defense will now present their case for acquittal before the court.

When Defense Counsel Flynn rises and announces that his first defense witness will be Jonathan Anderson, the twin brother of the defendant, Randolph Anderson, the prosecutor jumps to his feet and objects to this surprise witness. He claims that the state never received due notice of this witness nor did they have an opportunity to question this witness prior to his testifying.

Judge Folger pounds his gavel and declares that the State's objection was overruled. Jonathan may testify.

Randolph is astounded by the sight of Jonathan, his long-despised twin brother. "My God," he ponders as he views his brother before him, "he really is my twin brother. Amazing." Randolph wonders how his miserable brother is going to help his case. He thinks, *He'll probably seal my fate and help the state falsely convict him.*

Attorney Flynn approaches Jonathan and asks, "What is your relationship with the defendant?"

Jonathan proceeds to explain their long and tattered journey through their childhood and into adulthood, including the many years of animosity. He then explains his improvement in his health and coincidently, Irene's contact with him. At first, Jonathan couldn't figure out why she did contact him and why she was so cordial to him. The terrible auto accident had occurred only a few weeks earlier.

At first, he thought she was seeking sympathy and compassion, but soon thereafter, he realized those were not her prime motives for courting his presence.

It became obvious to him that Irene was looking for a compatriot to share her hatred of his brother Randolph for the auto accident and the eventual death of her daughter. Jonathan explains that with his long-standing hatred of his brother Randolph, it was not difficult for Irene to subtly convince him to blame Randolph for the death of Irene's daughter, Erin.

Attorney Flynn then presents Jonathan's personal log to the court for identification and admission. Attorney Johnson promptly objects to the admission on the basis of it being fiction. Judge Folger denies the objection and the log is admitted.

Attorney Flynn has Jonathan explain the origin of the log and its development. Jonathan explains that over time he started to realize that Irene seemed to be using him to strengthen her blame positions. Almost everything that they did together or talked about was very anti-Randolph. It seemed like she was building a case against Randolph.

Jonathan thumbs through his personal log explaining each of his entries. As he completes his review, it becomes obvious that much of what was written could lead to the conviction of Irene. Randolph is innocent; Irene is the culprit.

Judge Folger calls for a recess and asks the two attorneys to join him in his chambers. When all three are seated in the judge's chambers, Judge Folger begins, "I believe we're heading in the wrong direction with this trial. Although I've no substantive proof, I believe that Randolph Anderson is an innocent man. And, further, I think that the real guilty party in this case is his wife, Irene Anderson. I propose that we suspend our present trial for the time being while I direct the District Attorney to reopen their investigation with emphasis on Irene Anderson as the prime suspect. If this expanded investigation proves conclusively that Irene Anderson is the guilty party, we will dismiss the present charges against Randolph and file similar charges against Irene Anderson."

Both prosecuting and defense counsels are incredulous. Neither had ever experienced such an action in the middle of a trial. Nonetheless, they greatly respect Judge Folger and pledge to cooperate.

When the case is referred back to the DA's office, Detective James Sullivan is reassigned to the case as the chief investigative officer. His mission is to reopen the Randolph Anderson investigation with prime interest on Irene Anderson.

Detective Sullivan enthusiastically accepts the challenge. He will review all the prime evidence in their custody to see if Irene Anderson better fits the role of prime suspect. His first endeavor is to carefully review all the physical evidence already filed in the evidence room. He signs out fourteen boxes of evidence for review.

As he examines the two storage boxes taken from Randolph Anderson's bedroom closet, he recalls that two sets of fingerprints were recovered from the tape used to seal the two cardboard boxes. The enclosed forensic lab's report identifies the owners of the prints. One set belonged to Randolph Anderson and the other to Irene Anderson. Sullivan muses to himself, "Why would her prints be on the wrapping tape unless she actually packed the case?"

And that's the box that contained the incriminating evidence at its bottom. It sure looks like a case of key evidence being planted by a guilty party to throw investigators off the track. Sullivan is quite pleased with his discovery. Reexamining the items found at the bottom of the box in Randolph's closet, he lifts up the baseball cap and looks it over carefully. This time he notices a blond hair on the inside lining of the cap. He places it into an evidence bag and brings it up to the lab for identification as human or artificial. The next day, he is informed that the blond hair strand is not human but artificial as in a wig. The evidence against Irene Anderson is growing.

Sullivan's next stop is the Anderson House. He calls Sue Greene for permission to visit with her on Saturday morning. Sullivan shows up and is greeted by Sue. Sue is curious and asks why they are reopening the case. Sullivan explains the situation to Sue who offers, "I never believed that Randolph was guilty of any of those charges. Actually, in the months before the trial, Irene had become almost a maniac with her protestations of hatred toward Randolph. If nothing else, Irene sure had a strong motive to implicate her husband. Also, she seemed to be losing her long-term battle with bipolar disorder." Sullivan made a special note of that little tidbit.

He thanks her for her insight. He then moves on to the two alleged attempts on Irene's life. Sue quickly responds, "I never did believe that Randolph set up those attempts. Actually, from the very beginning, I felt that Irene had arranged both incidents to cast suspicion on her husband. Since I was intimately involved in both incidents, I was always suspicious of the timing in both cases. With the garage door and carbon monoxide attempt, Irene had arranged to meet me at six o'clock at her home. Irene knows that I am an on-time nut. That day, I did arrive exactly on time and purportedly saved her life."

Sue continues, "The swimming pool incident also took place while I was visiting Irene. Sue seemed to arrange things so that I was the first to get to the pool and notice the portable radio at the bottom of the pool. When she heard me yell out, Irene ran over behind the pool shrubbery and supposedly unplugged the extension line."

Sullivan asks if he could take another look at the pool. Sue agrees and states, "Actually, it's just about the way it was on that day. I did remove the radio from the pool, but I left the electric extension cord as it was."

Sullivan heads out to the pool and sees the extension cord extending out of the pool into the shrubs. He follows the line to the electrical panel box next to the pool's water heater and its filter.

His basic understanding of electricity matters tells him that all electrical circuits near a water source, as in this case, should be protected by a ground fault circuit interrupter (GFCI). They're like super fast circuit breakers that trip at the first sign of a malfunction. They can usually be recognized by a test button and a reset button. Sullivan notes that the two outlet plugs available for use with the radio's extension cord both were tripped and therefore were dead circuits. "Accordingly, a radio in the pool never did pose a life threat to anyone."

When Sue hears that, she says, "That clinches it. In both attempts on her life, there was no real risk. And now I finally believe she was well aware of that." Sullivan thanks Sue for her cooperation and leaves.

CHAPTER TWENTY-NINE

Detective Sullivan, armed with a fast-developing arsenal of evidence against Irene, prepares and submits a sworn affidavit requesting the right to search Irene Anderson's house for further evidence. Within a few days, he is granted the requested search warrant. He contacts Sue to arrange for a convenient day to conduct the search. They agree on the upcoming Saturday at 10:00 AM.

Upon arrival, he and his associate proceed to conduct a thorough search of the premises. Sullivan enters a bedroom that obviously once was Irene's daughter's room. The room is beautifully decorated with lots of dolls and an array of pictures of Erin in various costumes. Sullivan notes that one of the photographs pictured Erin in a witch's costume replete with a ragged blond wig.

Sullivan locates the witch costume in a plastic sleeve in the closet. He removes the wig and bags it as evidence. When he returns to his office, he delivers the wig to the forensic lab to determine if the strand from the baseball cap matches up with the wig. Sure enough, it's a match. *Another nail in Irene's coffin, muses Sullivan*. The "man" who was dressed in black coveralls and wore a black baseball cap and was identified in the Caruso Company's parking lot was most probably Irene in disguise. She even wore the blond wig to look more like Randolph. That seems like a given, seeing that neither Randolph nor Jonathan had to wear a blond wig; nature took care of that.

With his success on the fingerprints left on Randolph's packing boxes, Sullivan recalls collecting prints from the envelope and birthday card presented to C. C. at her birthday party. He recalls that two sets were found but couldn't be identified since they weren't on file with the national computer fingerprint base. Now he has the lab compare Irene's prints with those on the birthday card and envelope. Again, they find a match. It follows that Irene Anderson is linked to the kidnapping and killing as well as the delivery of the dead cat at the birthday party for C. C., the nine-year-old daughter of the Carusos.

And now with Jonathan Anderson providing first-person testimony of Irene visiting the Carusos' nursery and exiting with a handbag over her shoulder, Sullivan's case strengthens. She had adequate time to spread the poisonous powder on the soil in the iris section of the garden. The fact that she misled the Carusos' gate guard into thinking she and Jonathan were really Mr. and Mrs. Anderson clearly shows an intent to implicate her husband as the guilty party.

With Sue Greene's testimony on how Irene's mental state had deteriorated over the past six months, Sullivan decides to visit with her long-term doctor, Dr. Jensen. At first, Dr. Jensen was reluctant to discuss intimate details of Irene's mental condition. He did relent when he was informed that Irene was involved in a manslaughter case where she is the prime suspect. Sullivan explains that her mental capacity might be her only defense. Dr. Jensen opens up a bit and explains that Irene is suffering from an advanced case of bipolar disorder, which can cause severe mood swings. Detective Sullivan asks the doctor if someone with BPD, in an extreme mood shift, could cause harm to someone else. Dr. Jensen hesitates and responds, "I believe they might."

Detective Sullivan returns to his office and begins preparing a formal investigation report for submission to his boss, DA Hayes. After a comprehensive study of the report and much discussion, DA Hayes decides to bring Irene in and confront her with the damning evidence they possess.

Irene is ushered into the DA's interrogation room where DA Hayes and Detective Sullivan are waiting for her at a conference table. The DA opens with "Mrs. Anderson. Thank you for coming in. As you know, we're still investigating the many felonies perpetrated against the Caruso family as well as the manslaughter charge in the death of Janet Zook. Since you are a suspect in these cases, I'm going to read you your Miranda Rights. Are you amenable to that?"

Irene squirms a bit in her chair and quietly answers, "I don't care, go ahead and read them to me."

Once the rights were read and acknowledged, DA Hayes gets right into it, "Mrs. Anderson, we believe that you were responsible for all these crimes, including the death of the Carusos' neighbor, Janet Zook. And we have irrefutable evidence to back up our case against you."

Irene is visibly shaken. She rises from her seat and yells, "What? You couldn't pin those crimes on my rotten husband, so now you're coming after me. He's the one who should pay for killing my precious daughter. I gave you all the evidence you needed to hang him, but you guys all stick together. He should be on death row by now. The bastard."

DA Hayes interrupts Irene's rant, "Are you admitting that you are responsible for all of these offenses just to get even with your husband?" Irene stares right into the DA's eyes and replies, "Yes, I do. I knew you guys would never hold my rotten husband responsible for killing my daughter, so I had to do what I had to do."

DA Hayes settles her down and asks her to put her confession in writing. He hands her a pad of paper and a pen. Irene grabs them and starts to write.

Hayes and Sullivan leave her alone in the interrogation room. Irene is watched through a special one-way glass panel. After about an hour, Irene stops writing and tosses the pen and pad against the door. An attendant enters the room and retrieves the pad. Almost every page is filled with *Bastard, Murder, Killer, Erin*, and other words of hate.

The DA has Irene booked for the various charges and placed in a cell. He orders a psychiatric examination of Irene to determine her present mental state and to determine if she is sane enough to stand trial.

~

After an extensive battery of psychiatric tests and hours of interviews with several experienced psychiatrists, a formal report is prepared and submitted to DA Hayes and Judge Folger on the basis of the psychiatrist's reports, which concluded that Irene Anderson is not in her right mind and is not capable of understanding the criminality of her actions or their magnitude. Judge Folger calls her before him and explains that he finds her responsible for all the alleged charges. Rather than sending her to prison where she would have little chance of recovery, he is ordering her confined at the NY State Psychiatric Center at New Paltz for a term of at least ten years or until she is judged to be mentally sound and not a threat to herself or others.

Judge Folger then dismisses all charges against Randolph Anderson. He is immediately released from custody.

~

Charles Caruso and Bruce Byrnes, Caruso Construction Company's VP of Municipal Bidding and Contracting Services, arrive at the Garden City Inn for the annual award banquet of the Long Island Construction Company Association (LICCA).

The LICCA and its corporate members gather each year for their award banquet to recognize and honor outstanding community contributions on the part of their members.

Charles and Bruce are directed to table 12, which is located in front of the head table. There are eight other members at their table. After seating, Charles rises and introduces himself and Bruce. After the next six members introduce themselves, a well-dressed man rises and introduces himself as Joseph Bianco, president of Granite Construction.

It's hard to tell who is more surprised at that pronouncement. Charles can't believe that his current archenemy is seated next to him. Joseph Bianco seems nonplussed by the coincidence.

As the evening ceremonies wear on and the Chianti and conversation flows between the two *paisanos*, Joseph leans over to Charles and says, "We got off to a poor start. I'd really like to have you visit my operation one of these days. I think a bonding of our companies could be mutually beneficial. Here's my business card. Give me a call."

Charles seizes the moment and responds, "That makes sense. I'll have my secretary call your office and set up a date." They shake hands and smile.

They enjoy the presentation of awards and a fine six-course meal.

Brian is amazed at the turn of events. Who could have predicted such a radical outcome? That's amore!

~

"The Lord doth work in strange and mysterious ways."

~

Driving home from the LICCA Banquet, Charles does some serious soul-searching. After all he and his family have endured during the past year, he wonders if he wants to anticipate an unpredictable future. His wife, Carmella, is still heartbroken over the tragic death (murder) of her friend and neighbor, Janet Zook. And she just can't get started on a new nursery/garden at their home in Harborport. The very ground seems evil to her and should remain barren. C. C., their precious daughter, is still shaken by her horrible experiences of the past year, especially with Fluffy and her birthday party.

And Chip has moved out of their home and is in the process of developing his own life apart from his family.

If Charles wants to make a move vis-à-vis his personal and professional priorities, now might be the appropriate time. Rather than acting hastily, he decides to confer with his trusted counsel, Donald Langsford, and broach the subject of a major relocation with him. Charles will call him in the morning to get the process rolling.

After further deliberation over the possibility of a drastic shift in his private and professional priorities, Charles places a call to Langsford and explains his dilemma. He arranges for a conference with Donald and Charles's trusted accountant, Ralph Barlow. They will meet at Donald's office on Wednesday at two o'clock.

Charles opens the meeting with an explanation of his ambivalence regarding his continued involvement with Caruso Construction as well as his family remaining in Harborport. The first subject they tackle is the sale of Caruso Construction. Charles mentions that Joseph Bianco recently expressed a passing interest in acquiring his company.

The alternative to a presumably fast sale to a known associate is to place the company sale with a respected local business broker. This process can be prolonged and exasperating as various potential "lookers" review the proposition, each from their own priorities and conditions.

After a lengthy discussion of the first two options, CPA Barlow suggests a different approach. He proposes consideration of transferring a significant portion of Charles's company stock into an ESOP plan. "That's an Employee Stock Ownership Plan in which you pass ownership of a major portion of your stock to your trusted employees through a stock-purchase program. For your protection, you would still maintain ownership rights. With ownership, employees are encouraged to represent your company better and work harder. Local banks usually provide reasonable credit to employees for their initial stock purchase."

Charles expresses great interest in the ESOP program and asks Ralph to prepare a detailed outline of the plan and how it could be implemented. Donald also endorses this approach.

The three men agree to meet again the following week to complete the details of the ESOP plan and to implement it. Charles is most pleased with their decision.

CHAPTER THIRTY

It's December 31, and Chip is ready for a big night to celebrate the end of the old year and the dawning of hopefully a more successful and rewarding year for him. The old year was pretty rough on him. He just did dodge a serious DUI rap, though he did get hit with a staggering $3,000 fine.

Then he was charged in that stupid break-in and vandalism of his parents' home in Stony Pines. That stupidity cost him his pristine criminal record and another mammoth fine of $2,000. That's the fine the Stony Pines court imposed on him after he pled guilty to the break-in and vandalism charges. Those two fines made short shrift of his college graduation gift fund.

On the bright side, he did get away with another of his antics during the year. He was able to partially avenge that arrogant damn professor who swore he would kill him at the professor's daughter's funeral. All that after Chip was nice enough to attend the funeral and pay his respects.

Setting those metal railroad spikes in that hotshot bastard's Cadillac Escalade's four tires was sheer genius. Chip wishes he could have waited around the professor's driveway that morning to witness his reaction to seeing four punctured Michelin tires.

Still, in spite of his many misadventures during the year, Chip came through it pretty much unscathed. Of course, his father still resents him and probably will for a long time to go.

Thank the good Lord, Chip's position with National Brands has panned out real well. He's been named Associate of the Month twice in the last four months. That position with Caruso Construction probably won't be coming down the pike for quite a while, if then.

So, all in all, Chip was pretty fortunate to have survived the year and avoid jail time. His plan for this last day of the year is to really enjoy this New Year's Eve and to herald in the New Year with a bang.

In mid-December, Chip was surprised by a call on his cell phone from Lucy Thieman. Lucy was one of those summertime romances of several years ago when he spent most of his summer months in Stony Pines at his parents' house. Lucy's parents also owned a gorgeous summer retreat in Stony Pines, not far from the Carusos' home. It was one of those summertime flirtations that Chip had not forgotten.

Lucy had called to invite him to join her as her date at a gala New Year's Eve party at her parents' home in Stony Pines. Chip gladly accepts her totally unexpected invitation. He tells her that he is very much looking forward to renewing their relationship.

On New Year's Eve, Chip leaves Rego Park and heads out to Stony Point via the Long Island Expressway. The trip should take about an hour or so. He should arrive around ten thirty.

The skies are cloudy and the forecast is for light rain and freezing temperatures.

Chip arrives on schedule, and after reestablishing his relationship with Lucy, now a beautiful young lady, he joins in with the other partygoers. There's lots of music, eats, and an open bar.

Between dances with Lucy, Chip manages to down a few Bacardi and Cokes, his favorite.

The bewitching hour arrives and Chip and Lucy embrace and exchange kisses. Chip is really enjoying Lucy's company again. And she seems to share that sentiment too.

By two o'clock, Chip is feeling pretty good. The combination of the wiles of Lucy and the kick of his favorite drink sees to that. Chip decides it would be prudent to call it an evening and head back to Rego Park. Maybe he is maturing. Chip thanks Lucy for a great evening, gives her a kiss and a hug, and promises to call her real soon.

Chip gets into his company car and heads down Route 23W, which will connect him with the Long Island Expressway. The cold rain has changed to sleet, and Chip feels his car reacting to the slippery road conditions. Being a macho guy, he isn't deterred; he motors on.

Route 23W is a two-lane highway that winds along the coastline of Suffolk County.

Tonight it's fairly treacherous driving due to the existence of "black ice," a dangerous road condition caused by a thin, almost invisible coating of glazed ice on the surface of a road. The color of the road below the ice layer shows through, allaying a driver's concern.

Chip has no idea of the perils lurking ahead of him around the next bend in the road. As he approaches a sudden hairpin curve in the road, he hits a patch of black ice and his car spins uncontrollably onto the road's shoulder, ramming through the metal guard railing, causing the car to flip over and crash into a stand of established pine trees.

Chip, who isn't wearing his seat belt, is sent flying headfirst into his windshield. On impact, he instantly loses consciousness as he is suspended upside down in the wreck of his car.

Soon another car passing by sees the smoldering wreck and calls 911. Within minutes, an NY state trooper pulls up in his patrol cruiser. Surveying the wreck and noting that the driver is still trapped in the car in an unconscious state, he calls for an EMS response and the local fire department, requesting they respond with their "jaws of life" equipment.

The EMS teams attempts to stabilize Chip until the fire department truck arrives to extricate him from the wreck. Soon the firemen arrive with their mechanical jaws of life. They cut through the mangled wreck and remove Chip from his car.

Chip is rushed to North Central Hospital where he is immediately diagnosed with traumatic brain injury (TBI) and facial trauma. He is sent directly to the ICU wing for MRI scanning and emergency surgery.

The hospital staff contacts his parents to inform them of their son's accident and hospitalization. Upon notification, the Carusos quickly dress and head out to the hospital.

~

Randolph almost can't believe that his long-despised twin brother came to his rescue in court today. It was Jonathan's revealing testimony that turned Randolph's trial on its head. Without Jonathan's testimony, Randolph was sure to end up with a conviction.

After much deep thought, Randolph finally decides to call Jonathan and express his heartfelt thanks for his life saving testimony. He calls Sunnyvale Meadows and asks to be connected to Jonathan's room. Jonathan answers the call and is somewhat shocked to find his long-hated twin brother on the line. He's momentarily speechless.

Randolph begins, "Jonathan, I just wanted to call and personally thank you rescuing me in court today. To show my appreciation and to renew our brotherhood, I'd like to invite you out for a special dinner. I'd really like to explore the chances of us becoming real brothers again. We both were used by Irene, and now she's gone. What do you say to joining me for dinner this coming Saturday night?"

Jonathan thinks for a minute and responds, "We've wasted too many years being jerks. Let's give our friendship a new beginning."

"Great. I'll check out a nice restaurant in your area and make a reservation."

Both brothers smile into their phones. Jonathan adds, "See you then, brother."

~

Irene is settled in the court-ordered NY State Psychiatric Center at New Paltz. She is assigned a semiprivate room in the observation ward with 24/7 monitoring. Her new medications seem to be addressing her mental issues as well as her feelings of revenge and hate. Her night terrors have abated, and she is sleeping quietly. Of course, she doesn't understand why she in this institution. It was all one big accident. Life sucks.

Ironically, the Psychiatric Center at New Paltz is the very same institute that her husband's twin brother was confined to when he had that swing set accident all those years ago.

CHAPTER THIRTY-ONE

After enjoying his newfound freedom for several days, Randolph turns his attention to the lawsuit filed against the Carusos. He calls Raymond Cotter, their attorney who is handling the lawsuit for them, and sets an appointment for the next day.

The first issue they discuss is Randolph's trial and its outcome. Randolph asks, "With Irene being institutionalized, how does that affect our upcoming trial with the Carusos?" Cotter replies, "We will have to refile our lawsuit with you being the lone plaintiff. That will put the trial off a few weeks."

~

Meanwhile, at Donald Langsford's offices, Charles Caruso is being informed of Irene's situation, "With her mental state now on the record, it certainly bolsters our case," opines Langsford. "On the other hand, Chip's auto accident and long-term hospitalization lends credence to the plaintiffs' argument about Chip's drinking problem. All in all, I believe that our hand has been strengthened by these events. Our firm and the insurance company agree that now would be a good time to request a court-supervised settlement conference to pound out an out-of-court settlement of the lawsuit." "How much are you thinking about?" asks Charles. Langsford replies, "We believe their side has been damaged the most. As you recall, the insurance investigation at the time of the accident assessed the other party with 78 percent of the blame for the accident. Now with the disclosure about Irene Anderson's poor mental condition, I believe that their share of blame is now in the mideighties. Now seems like the right time to petition Judge Redmond to call for a settlement conference between the two parties."

He goes on, "We estimate that the Andersons incurred somewhere in the range of fifty thousand dollars and a hundred thousand dollars in hospital and burial expenses for their daughter plus automobile repair costs. We think that we would start with an offer of fifty thousand dollars and be willing to accept the higher limit. What do you think?"

Charles responds, "The sooner we can get past this matter, the better. Let's proceed with the settlement conference."

~

Raymond Cotter receives notification of the date for a settlement conference. He calls Randolph and asks him to come into Cotter's office to discuss the settlement conference requested by the Carusos. That evening, he arrives at Cotter's office.

Cotter begins, "Obviously the other side has been informed of Irene's diagnosis and confinement. They must feel that our position has been greatly weakened and now would be a good time to settle." Randolph chimes in, "How much do you think they will offer to settle?"

Cotter responds, "A lot less than what we are demanding in the lawsuit. I would think they would try to get out of this matter for a hundred thousand dollars or so." Randolph asks, "What's our chances of getting a lot more than that?"

After pondering the question for a few minutes, Cotter opines, "If you recall, that insurance report assigned 68 percent of the responsibility for the accident on us. And now with the new Irene disclosure, that percentage should go higher. I think if we are offered a hundred thousand dollars, we should take it."

The settlement conference begins in Judge Redmond's chambers as scheduled. After a few opening remarks by the judge, each side is requested to briefly present its argument for their suggested settlement amount. Raymond Cotter leads off and presents his case largely on the back of Chip Caruso's alcohol problem. Donald Langsford follows and bases his argument on the original insurance analysis of blame for each party. At the time of the accident, 68 percent of the blame fell on the Anderson's backs. Now with the disclosure that Irene Anderson, the other driver, suffered from bipolar disorder at the time of the accident, over 80 percent of the blame and responsibility should reside with the Andersons.

The judge asks each side several pertinent questions and then asks each party to write an acceptable settlement figure on a piece of paper, fold it and hand it to him. Judge Redmond reviews both figures and announces that the final settlement figure will be seventy-five thousand dollars.

Stoically, both parties rise, thank the judge, and file out of his chambers.

EPILOGUE

New Year's Eve, three years later, and much has changed in the lives of our characters.

Charles Caruso, frustrated by that year of contentiousness, fear, and family upset, has sold his majority interest in Caruso Construction Company Inc. Initially, it appeared that Joseph Bianco, Charles's new business associate, was leading the bidders. But Charles felt that such a drastic change in ownership would jeopardize Caruso Construction's proud reputation for quality and fair dealing. Any Mafia connection would surely taint their fine name and standing in the industry.

Instead, Charles opted for a 401 ESOP (Employee Stock Ownership Plan) program that enables company employees to purchase ownership in their company. Such a plan guarantees continuity for all involved and encourages greater company loyalty.

With the ownership of their company settled, Charles and Carmella moved on to the next phase of their family reestablishment. Together they researched the luxury real-estate market in beautiful Coral Springs, Florida. They eventually settled on a majestic eight-thousand-square-foot mansion located on the Intercoastal Waterway. Charles is in the process of purchasing a forty-foot yacht. He plans on spending a fair amount of his now free time pursuing deep-sea fishing.

Carmella is enthused with the estate's pristine greenhouse and quarter-acre flower garden. Her dreams have been answered. She is looking forward to her new horticultural adventure.

Before Charles and Carmella closed on their new home in sunny Florida, they visited five private girls' academies. C. C. was given a priority position in the school selection process. She is very excited about being so involved in picking out her next school. Eventually, C. C. is enrolled at St. Martha's Academy for Girls. She is looking forward to her new school and making new friends.

Chip Caruso has made little progress in recovering from the severe head injuries sustained in his car accident. Charles, despite his disappointment in Chip's actions and attitude before his accident, arranged for Chip's transportation down to Florida and placement in a nearby psychiatric center so the family can visit and support him in his long recovery ordeal.

Jonathan and Randolph's weekly dinners and their lengthy discussions brought the two brothers close together. Randolph invited Jonathan to share his house with him. Jonathan graciously accepted his brother's invitation and moved in with him. Subsequently, Jonathan accepted an administrative position with the Nassau County Public Health Department in Mineola.

Once settled in their home, the brothers reached out to their extended family and now enjoy family relationships.

~

Sue Greene, Irene's long-term friend, still hasn't recovered from the courtroom theatrics and disclosures, particularly concerning Irene's malfeasance. As the sole occupant of Irene and Randolph's house, she felt it imperative to move out as soon as possible and reestablish herself in a fresh new environment. Accordingly, Sue resigned her position with Metro Research Inc. and moved back to Wellesley, Massachusetts. Once secure in her own lodgings, she solicits and accepts an administrative position in the admissions office at Wellesley College, where she and Irene graduated years ago.

~

Irene remains institutionalized with little to no progress noted over the past three years. Her rants and screaming fits are daily happenings. Most of her fellow patients avoid her presence as much as possible. The constant theme of her outbursts is her hatred of her bastard husband and that rotten Caruso kid.

~

Coco Crandel's reputation as a private investigator has been enhanced through the work performed on behalf of the various Caruso issues. His firm is sought out by many individuals and companies.

"Revenge is an act of passion; resistance of justice. One good act of vengeance deserves another. The Lord's word be done."

Edwards Brothers,Inc!
Thorofare, NJ 08086
22 March, 2011
BA2011081